GIRL
MEETS
BOY

GIRL MEETS BOY

BECAUSE THERE ARE
TWO SIDES TO EVERY STORY

EDITED BY KELLY MILNER HALLS

chronicle books · san francisco

Library of Congress Cataloging-in-Publication Data available.

ISBN 978-1-4521-0264-1

Manufactured in China.

Book design by Amelia May Mack.

Typeset in Sentinel.

10 9 8 7 6 5 4 3 2 1

This product conforms to CPSIA 2008.

Chronicle Books LLC

680 Second Street, San Francisco, California 94107

www.chroniclebooks.com/teens

TABLE OF CONTENTS

INTRODUCTION

What Was He / She Thinking?

As a kid, I was my family's "tomboy." My sister had staked her claim on being the "girly girl." Tomboy was the only choice left, but it suited me. I loved sports, getting dirty, and catching animals; my best friends were always boys.

As a teenager, the tomboy experience landed me in a realm of odd confusion. At last bonded with female friends too, I hardly recognized the heartless, narrow-minded boys they often described. The girls my guy friends talked about seemed just as cruel, shallow, and strange.

I realized—early on—truth is often subjective. Perception colors human reactions. If something happens, and two people were witnesses—one male and one female—their descriptions of the event might differ significantly, even if they were both determined to tell the truth.

Do you ever wonder, "What was that guy (or that girl) thinking?"

I was considering that question one night when it came to me. What if a group of authors took on the challenge of perception—boys versus girls? What if one writer wrote a story from a male or female point of view, then another writer of the opposite gender told the same story from the other character's perspective?

Girl Meets Boy represents the fascinating fruit of that literary labor. Twelve writers, paired to explore the differences and similarities.

Chris Crutcher wrote his story of a funny, great-looking jock falling for a dangerous girl first. I responded as the toxic girl who might never learn how to be loved. Cynthia Leitich Smith created her fearless, Native American basketball star. Joseph Bruchac introduced her to the tender, artistic boy she never knew she wanted. James Howe wrote about a gay boy aching to fall in love. Ellen Wittlinger revealed the girl who might help make it happen. Terry Trueman explored a white boy's crush on a fine African American young woman. Rita Williams-Garcia went back and forth on giving that player a shot. Terry Davis gave us a glimpse of a Bangladeshi boy trying to survive in Iowa. Rebecca Fjelland Davis's farm girl found an ally in the Islamic boy she soon came to love. And finally, Sara Ryan and Randy Powell revealed why romance wasn't an option for a very compelling girl and boy.

"Each pair of stories in this anthology is about bridging the gap of gender-based misunderstanding that can happen between girls and boys with the most reliable of human structures—the truth," said author Terry Davis. "Each team of writers deftly illustrates the courage required to ask, 'What is really happening here?' and, more important, to ask why."

With those two informational tools—the "what" and the "why"—real enlightenment is attainable. And when both genders (both races, both countries, both political parties, both sides of any disagreement) find enlightenment, they discover they're different in some ways, but heart-linked by sameness in many, many more.

LOVE
OR SOMETHING LIKE IT

by Chris Crutcher

My name is John Smith, and though I'm aware that an overwhelming number of men use my name to check in to motels they shouldn't be checking in to, I try to be a man of virtue. Okay, I'm sixteen; a boy of virtue. On the surface, with one exception, I couldn't seem more average if I lived in Kansas and drove my Ford Taurus to my job at the John Deere dealership five days a week. I'm five feet ten and a half inches tall with dark brown hair and light brown eyes. I weigh a hundred fifty-three pounds. My grade point average is a 2.5 out of a possible 4.0, and I've never had a grade lower than a D+ or higher than a B. Average guys should be calling me average. But I said there was one exception, and this is it: My face is so handsome it hurts. If *People* magazine knew I existed, they'd swarm this town like bumblebees on a turned-over honey truck right before their "Beautiful People" issue came out.

It probably sounds like I'm bragging, and if I were most guys, I probably would be, but this thing is a curse because it turns me into one lying son of a bitch. And I hate myself when I lie. I grew up going to Sunday school, learning the Ten Commandments and the Golden Rule; got a snoot full of the wrath of God from the Old Testament and the kinder, but just-as-firm, teachings of Jesus from the New Testament. They taught me that bad things happen if you lie and you stand a better chance of getting to heaven if you don't. My sixth-grade teacher was also the pastor of our church, and he was one no-nonsense kind of dude, the kind of guy who knows the true meaning of the word *smite*. In church he called them commandments and in school he called them rules, but the bottom line was, whether they were prefaced by "Thou Shalt Not" or "You'd Damn Well Better," they were written in stone and were to be followed.

I have no problem with that, seriously. There's nothing in the Ten Commandments that, under most circumstances, won't make you a better person. Under most circumstances, you shouldn't be killing people and you shouldn't be taking their stuff, and it would probably be in your best interest if you weren't having wet dreams about their wives or girlfriends, much less acting on those dreams. It probably doesn't help you much to covet their stuff, either. I admit it's hard to get behind not taking the Lord's name in vain; that one should probably be demoted from a commandment to a suggestion. I mean, if there is going to be hell to pay for breaking commandments, it doesn't seem right that a guy who cusses should pay the same hell as a rapist or murderer.

But I digress, because this isn't as much about my belief system as it is my integrity, which goes right out the window every time I get involved with a girl. As I said, I have learned that lying is a bad thing. I don't cheat on my homework anymore, and I don't shoplift like I did for about a month there in grade school, filling my pockets with SweeTarts and Tootsie Pops. If a cop stops me and asks if I know how fast I was going, I tell him. When my football coach asks if I followed the summer workout regimen, out comes the truth, whether it means running a mile after practice every day or not.

But when any of my old girlfriends asked if I was ever attracted to anyone else, I looked her right in the eye with an expression that said, *"ME?!"* and told her unequivocally she was the *only* one I *ever* thought of. I mean, I spoke in italics. Now, for reasons I may or may not go into here, I was a virgin each and every time I told that whopper, so while I wasn't breaking the adultery commandment, I was setting records alone in my room coveting to beat the band, and whatever else. At first that would be as far as it went, but then (and I hate to say it, but it's because I'm so darn good-looking) some girl who was also into coveting would come along and start telling me her problems, because I seem to have a sign on my flawless forehead that says "Tell Me How Awful Your Life Is, and I Will Save You" (which I have since been told comes from having an alcoholic mother), and I would set about saving her. Only the next thing I'd know, we'd make some secret unspoken agreement that the best way to save her was to have my hands all over her and my tongue in her mouth. I guess maybe my behavior around my current girlfriend would change because *she'd* start asking more and more often if I ever thought about anyone else, and then it would turn into was I *messing* with anyone else and, well . . . eventually, the girl followed my integrity right out that window. When I turned around to lick my self-inflicted wounds, guess what? There was another girl waiting. To my credit, I didn't jump right into a relationship with the first girl in line. Sometimes I'd wait as much as a week.

So I wanted to do the next one differently. I figured there had to be some kind of science to it; the idea of random mate selection probably wasn't a good one. If I wanted to know about fish, I'd see a marine biologist, right? If I wanted to know about space, as in the universe, I'd ask an astrophysicist. So, I thought, who would be the scientists when it comes to this love thing?

Counselors, that's who. Therapists. Psychologists. Only I didn't know any counselors or therapists or psychologists, except for "Mrs. Don't-Take-It-Out-for-Anything-but-Urinary-Relief Hartson," our school counselor. So the next best thing would be to go to someone who had *been* to one. Doesn't that make sense?

Maybe on paper.

Her name was, and still is, Wanda Wickham, and she was sharper than the piece of glass she keeps in her purse to cut on her arms with. She was sixteen and had been in five foster placements in the past three years. She wasn't very tall, maybe just over five feet, and built like . . . Well, put it this way: If you were part of the crowd streaming out of Sodom and Gomorrah right behind Lot's wife, and you *saw* Lot's wife look back and turn into a pillar of salt, and Wanda Wickham was back there waving a handkerchief and cooing your name, you'd look back, too. Instant deer lick, but you'd look.

So in the beginning I was just going to use her for deep background, you know? I mean, she'd been in trouble every day she'd been to school, which was about fifty percent of the time, telling off teachers or breaking the dress code in ways that sent most of us guys home sentenced to night sweats. It was that or getting into physical altercations with girls who had to slap their boyfriends' slack jaws shut every time Wanda "accidentally" rubbed up against them in the lunch room or out by the lockers. I figured *some*thing had to be keeping her out of alternative school, and I figured that something was more than likely a good shrink.

I was right.

I didn't have to seek her out, really. Wanda and I were well acquainted. My last girlfriend, Nancy Hill, had barely escaped a three-day suspension after I broke up a fight between her and Wanda. There had been an hour-long session in Mrs. Hartson's office following that fight, during which I had to back up Nancy's version of the story. Wanda sat across the counselor's office from me, just out of Mrs. Hartson's line of vision, running her fingernails over the soft rise in her tight sweater, a smile playing around her lips as she wet them with her tongue. I was in more trouble with Nancy *after* I bailed her out of a three-day vacation than I had been going in.

"So, Wanda," I said now, "what's going on?"

She closed her locker and held her books tight to her chest. "You're going on, Johnny Smith," she said. "You're always going on."

I said, "Listen, I'm doing a little research project, kind of a thing for psychology, and, uh, I wonder if you would . . . could . . . tell me . . . like, do you see a counselor, by any chance?"

Wanda put a finger to my nose. That should have been a warning, because what might be just a cute gesture coming from most girls was *electric* coming from Wanda. "You're doing a research project for *psychology* on me? I think you're doing a research project for *yourself* on me."

At that point I was a few days out of my last relationship, so I was trying to catch my lies before they did that geometric thing they do. "Actually, you're right," I said, and I told her my plan, which basically amounted to a poor man's way of talking to a psychologist. "So, do you? See a therapist?"

Wanda laughed. "I've seen more therapists in the last three years than our whole class has seen McDonald's workers. Tell me how I can help. *Damn* you are good-looking." She touched the side of my face.

I blushed and gave her my story in a nutshell. "Every time I get with a girl, I think I'm going to do it right this time. No matter what, I'm telling no lies, except for the necessary ones—you know, 'How do you like this blouse?' 'Do you like my hair this way?' Or 'Am I the best kisser you've ever kissed?'"

"Those are good questions to lie about, if you have to," she agreed. "How do you like *this* blouse?"

"This blouse" included about two inches of cleavage. I said it looked very nice.

"So how long does it take you to start lying?" she asked.

"Depends," I said. "If I like her a lot, not very long. The first lie is easy. It comes in response to her first question about how I feel; the minute I know how I really feel is not the way she wants me to feel. I can read that stuff like a book."

"Oooh." She laughed. "You are every needy girl's dream."

That is the line to which I should have paid maximum attention.

So Wanda Wickham and I made a deal. We would sit down once or twice a week, and I would vent a little history for her to run by her therapist. She'd come back and tell me her shrink's response—give me some free psychological advice. She had spent the last six months covering the same old territory in her own life and thought her therapist might enjoy the divergence. It *seemed* like such a good deal I was considering majoring in business when I go to college.

Think *bankruptcy.*

Our first meeting was at the Frosty Freeze only hours before her next appointment.

Wanda said, "So tell me about your mother."

"What?"

"Your mother. Tell me about your mother."

"Why would I tell you about my mother?"

"That's the first thing any therapist wants to know. Trust me. If I don't give her that information, she'll just tell me to come back and get it. Any therapist worth her salt has to know about your mother."

I felt like I did wearing that gown they gave me when I stayed overnight in the hospital having my tonsils out. My butt was exposed.

Well, nothing's free. "Let's see. She works as a checker at Walmart and cleans houses on her days off and on weekends. She does some of the light bookwork for my dad's business. She always has dinner ready on time and keeps the place cleaned up; you know, laundry and dishes and all that."

"Do she and your dad have sex?"

"I don't know! How would I know that? Your therapist would want to know that?"

She patted my hand. "Take it easy. People do that, you know. So, she works outside the home, cleans and does laundry, gets ignored by your dad. Does she have sex with you?"

I'm up. I mean, I'm *up.* Standing over Wanda, who looks at

me innocently. "What kind of question is that? What's the matter with you?"

She smiled, reached over, and patted my chair. "Sit down," she said. "I was just messing with you. That's the kind of thing therapists ask. Usually they wait quite a few sessions, though."

I stared at her.

"I was *kidding*."

I sat back down.

"Anything else?" she said. "About your mom, I mean."

"Well, she's an alcoholic."

That information didn't have much impact. "What kind?"

"What do you mean, 'what kind'? What kinds are there?"

"Lots. There are people who drink all the time, people who go on binges, people who only drink at certain times of the day—"

"That's my mom. She starts drinking when she starts making dinner. Goes to bed about nine. Actually, passes out about nine."

"Hmm. Workaholic and alcoholic. Tell you what. I can give you a little therapy without even asking Rita. I'll make some statements, and you tell me if they're right or wrong."

"Okay. Shoot."

"Your mom and dad don't talk to each other much."

She's right.

"Your mom's sad."

Right again. There's a pervasive sadness about my mother. Even when she's enjoying herself, she's sad under it.

"Your dad's distant."

"Meaning?"

"You never know how he feels. He just tells you—and your mother—how things are."

Right.

She looked into my eyes and squinted. "So when your mother feels bad enough, she tells *you* how she feels."

Whoa. She was so right I didn't even nod.

She put up her hands, palms out. "Don't answer," she said. "I know the answer to that one. And *you* try to make her life better. *You* tell her how cool she is and how good of a mom."

I wanted to ask her how the *hell* she knew that, but to tell the truth, I didn't want to know. I have always listened to my mother's woes for hours on end. The more she curses herself, the more I tell her how cool she is.

"Okay, then," she said cheerily. "I'm off for your therapy session. Wish me luck." She stopped at the door, turned back, and shook her head slowly. "God, but you are good-looking."

And that was the way it went. Wanda Wickham would sit with me in the Frosty Freeze and listen to the stories of my slow parade of girlfriends since age thirteen—none of whom liked me anymore—and take them back to Rita whatever-her-name-was. I don't remember much of her return advice, other than at one point she told me Rita said I was a very conscientious boy and it was good that I took care of my mother's emotional pain. Had I really known anything about therapy, that line alone would have told me trouble was brewing.

The problem was, as you might have already guessed, that I was paying less and less attention to what Wanda said to me and more and more attention to how she was dressed and what it felt like when she accidentally brushed my leg or pressed something soft against my elbow.

She was waiting for me at the Frosty Freeze when I got there after her—*our*—fourth or fifth session. "I'm sorry, Johnny," she said. "I think we're going to have to stop this."

"How come?"

"Well, I mean, what's in it for me? What do I get out of it? Look at you. You're going to figure out how to have a good relationship with a girl and go off and find one. Where does that leave me?" She stood up. Tears rimmed her eyes. God, I hadn't even thought this might be hard for her. Wanda Wickham traditionally went out with guys at least four years older. Guys in the army. Guys with kids. And wives. From a *heat* standpoint, she was so far out of my league we were playing a different sport.

I said, "Wait—"

"No," she said back. "I'm sorry. This isn't your fault. I didn't think I'd ... Fall in love."

WHAM!

In a court of law on trial for my life, I couldn't tell you what sequence of events took place in the following few minutes, but the next thing I remember we were kicking the windows out of my father's 1979 Chevy pickup from the inside and I had passed up double-A ball and triple-A ball and landed in the *majors*.

Wanda pulled her blouse back on and looked at me. Tears welled up. "Oh," she said. "What have I done now?"

"What do you mean? I think—"

"I don't give myself to a man unless I love him," she said. "But I promised myself that next time I wouldn't do it until he loved me back."

"Well, uh—"

"Don't," she said, putting two fingers to my lips. "I know you don't want to lie, and I don't want to hear any more lies. This wasn't your fault. I'll deal with it."

"But—"

"Shhh."

She was out of the pickup and gone.

I didn't see Wanda other than to pass her in the hall for almost a week. She would glance at me with a sad smile and turn away, and it scooped out my insides. The only thing I wanted more than a return engagement in the pickup was to make her feel better. Okay, maybe the pickup antics took over first place once in a while, but still, I had such a powerful urge to make her life better. Look what she had done for me. She'd befriended me, talked with me about my problems, even taken them to a professional. And she'd gone away feeling bad.

The only things I know that increased geometrically faster than my lies in an ill-fated relationship were my late-night and early-morning small-motor calisthenics before I was able to get close to Wanda again. I have heard it said that the adolescent male is in possession of two brains, and his capacity to be a decent human being is dependent on his capability to choose wisely when to use which. Well, that's a lie. There is no which. There is one brain. It is a ventriloquist, which is the *only* reason it ever even appears to come from the cranium.

I called Wanda. I asked her to meet me at the Frosty Freeze. I only wanted to make her feel better, I lied. She said she didn't trust herself to keep her hands off me. I lied again and said I would keep things under control. I wanted her to know she was cared about. I wanted her to know that all guys don't just want sex. (And in the end, I should say, that wasn't completely a lie. All guys don't *just* want sex. But all guys want sex.)

We met. She wore jeans and a blouse with an open sweater over it. The blouse buttoned at the top, but had an open circle just below the top button. Not a very big one, just big enough to make me visually fill in the blanks. She looked beautiful, but worn out,

23

beaten. I ordered us both a Coke and sat staring, feeling cautious about how to start. She smiled weakly, but let me stew, figure it out for myself.

"I'm really sorry," I started.

"You don't have to be sorry," she said. "It was my fault."

"I'm not sorry about *that*," I said. "I liked that. I liked it a lot. I'm just sorry you feel bad. I mean, I know you've had a hard life. The foster care and everything. Losing your parents and all."

"Yeah," she said. "I can't even tell you." And then she proceeded to tell me of drug-dealing biological parents who lived in a crack house and who were so strung out they let anyone who came and went have access to Wanda. Her dad went to jail, and her mom cleaned up three times before finally losing Wanda for good when she was seven. By then she'd already been in and out of foster care four times. She had attended thirteen schools total, had been sexually approached by teachers three different times. Three of her foster fathers had molested her, including the one she lived with now. Only she had threatened to kill this one in his sleep and he stopped. She just wanted the carnival to end, she said. She just wanted some peace. And she just wanted to be loved.

God, just hearing it made me love her, and I wanted to say that, but it seemed forced, like maybe it would feel like she was hurting too much, or looking for it. She smiled when I just sat there looking at her, not knowing what to say.

"Listen," she said. "I don't know how much longer I can take this, but I want you to promise me that if something happens, you won't blame yourself."

"Something happens," I said. "Like what?"

"Don't worry about it. Just promise me."

"Something like what?" I said. My agitation grew. Like when my mom was desperate to have my dad pay attention to her after dinner sometimes. She would wash the dishes with tears dripping off her nose, her rum and coke hidden in the cupboard next to the sink while he snored through *Law and Order* on the couch.

If anything ever happens to me, don't you blame yourself.

Anything happens? Like what?

Anything. Anything at all. And you make sure your father knows I love him.

"I said don't worry about it," Wanda said. "It isn't about you." She got up to leave.

I followed her out to her foster parents' car. She got in, placed both hands on the wheel, and stared ahead. A tear trickled down the side of her cheek.

"I do love you, Wanda," I said. "I mean, I think I really do. You haven't been off my mind for five minutes since I saw you last."

She turned her head and looked at me, smiling weakly. "You couldn't love me, Johnny." She's the only person who's ever called me Johnny. "Nobody could. There's nothing to love." She started the car and pulled out.

I jumped into the pickup and followed her, past my place, past hers, out to the river. She pulled into a wide spot hidden in the trees. I pulled in behind her, shut off the engine, walked over, and knocked on her window.

She rolled it down.

"I do love you, Wanda. I can prove it."

Best sex I ever had.

Course, I only had that one other time to compare to.

It's too late to make a long story short, but for a while, nothing could keep us apart. I picked her up for school and took her home.

I stopped going to intramural sports and dropped out of the music quartet I was practicing with to compete in the state music festival. I was able to give up those things that were once staples in my life as easily as a case of chicken pox so I could spend time with Wanda. Her foster mom thought I was the best thing in the world for her; she hadn't skipped a class since we started going together. Her caseworker and teachers were ecstatic because of her grades.

But as any relatively sane person knows, you can only breathe rare air so long before you need it to be mixed with the toxins that everyone else breathes. Caviar is great, but so is a burger. I'm not talking about other relationships here, not other girls. I'm talking about the things any stable human needs in his life to provide balance. Friends. Activities. A night alone watching TV. Time to let your *member* heal. You want to remember that I was a guy who, before I turned into a sex fiend, relieved myself a couple of times in the morning, a couple of times at night and once a day on a restroom break from Pre-Calc. I thought I held records. But Wanda Wickham wore me out. Sometimes we'd get done and I'd think I needed stitches in my back. And just *try* saying I was too tired or that I had to get homework done or that body fluids were finite. "Okay," she'd say. "I thought you loved me. I knew it would end. It always ends. Go ahead." Forty-five minutes later, I'd be driving home hoping I'd crash into a paramedic truck.

Suddenly I was on twenty-four-hour call. Wanda's panicked voice would breathe into my cell phone with increasing frequency. Fifteen-minute intervals, ten, five, three. Where was I? Had I been in a crash? Would I please call? Would I *please* call?

Then anger seeped in: What was I doing? Had I turned off my phone? *Why* had I turned off my phone? I was a lying son of a bitch. So it was going to end the way the others had.

The plain and simple truth, that I was sitting in my room, grabbing some minutes for myself, wondering who I was when I wasn't running to put out one of Wanda Wickham's fires, was *not* the answer she could tolerate, and I became a liar of Shakespearean status. My car broke down in an electronically dead place. My phone was lost, and I just found it. I *never* turned my phone off when I thought she might call. I didn't know why it went straight to voicemail; probably some glitch in AT&T. I thought of no other girls or women, *ever*. How could I?

Truth was, I was as smitten as the day I met her.

Before it was over, I had broken half the Commandments. No one died, but I stole my parents' pickup in the middle of the night to take her out to the river and hear the horrors of her foster father, who she always escaped, but who became more and more menacing. I had actually never met him because he worked long hours, and was never to even mention him to her foster mother, because Wanda could *not* afford to lose this placement. The last three times I snuck out after midnight it was to keep her from committing suicide. Nothing I did, no random act of kindness, no random act of desperation, made a dent.

So I went to see Rita the therapist.

"Hi," I said. "I'm John Smith. Thanks for seeing me."

Rita Crews had the same look on her face I always got the first time I said my name was John Smith.

"No, really," I said. "John Smith. I think you've probably heard my name."

She smiled. She was probably in her late fifties, smooth skin and shocking salt-and-pepper hair. "I've heard the name John Smith a lot," she said, "but until now, never in relation to a specific person."

I remembered. "You might know me as Johnny."

She looked pensive, shook her head.

"Wanda Wickham?"

No expression whatsoever.

"She's one of your clients."

"Confidentiality keeps me from telling you whether she is or isn't," Rita Crews said, "but I can assure you no one's mentioned your name in my office."

Whoa!

"Your ad said you do one consultation free," I said. "Is that a whole hour?"

"A whole hour," Rita said. "And let me give you some direction. Instead of using people's names and dates and times and places and all that, why don't you give me a hypothetical. I think I could answer your questions better if you could give me a hypothetical."

"Okay," I said. "Let's say there was this girl named Wendy Walkman . . ."

At the end of our freebie session, Rita Crews just smiled and shook her head. "How about instead of asking you a million questions, I just tell you what to do, and you do it," she said.

I'd have done *any*thing.

"Turn your cell phone off and leave it with me. I promise not to answer it. Call your girlfriend, whoever she may be, and tell her you're emotionally distraught and are calling off the relationship. Do not get into another one for one year. You can go out with friends, you can play sports and music, you can mix with boys and girls equally, but you cannot 'go' with anyone. Keep your offending member in your pants. Paste pictures of Britney and J.Lo on your ceiling and make passionate love to them to your heart's content. Then buy yourself a catheter if you have to and duct tape said offending member to your leg and padlock your zipper *shut*. Midnight to six in the privacy of your room is the *only* time it gets to breathe."

Can you believe that sounded good?

"And one more thing; when you think you have even the tiniest inkling why trying to save your mother and trying to save the hypothetical Wendy Walkman felt exactly the same, you call me and we'll go out for coffee. Okay?"

I thanked her as if she had led me to the Promised Land.

When I reached the door to her office, she said, "John?"

"Yeah."

"My goodness, you are a good-looking boy."

"I hate to say this," I said, "but I know it. And I'm scheduling plastic surgery for early next week."

SOME THINGS NEVER CHANGE

by Kelly Milner Halls

I was thirteen when I decided to tell my neighbor Andy my dirty little secret. Nose to nose between my foster mom's full-length rabbit coat and a thick row of her husband's coveralls—dizzy from the stink of man sweat and beer—I stepped outside of the box and took on a boy practically my own age.

"Turn on the flashlight," I whispered inside the overstuffed closet. "Cross your heart, swear to God you'll never breathe a word of this—to ANYONE." My blue polished nails made a cramped *X* across 34Cs. Andy Levine's flashlight gradually followed the trail. We're talking slow like the ice age; slow like Jim Carrey in *Dumb and Dumber*; slow like a really old geezer trying to get off.

"I swear on my mother's *grave*," he answered, his body bent, pinning the fur against the wall to keep from bumping his head.

"I'd swear on Jesus, if I thought it would get us out of this crappy closet. Why are we in here?"

"You're Jewish," I said, "Your *mommy* is next door, and I don't want to be interrupted. So swear on Moses or Hanukkah—or something like that. I mean it, Andy. If you want to hear the secret, you have to swear. It's totally juicy."

"Juicy like Wanda Wickham?" he asked, leering as I nodded. "Sweet! Then I swear on the Bar Mitzvah I never had. I swear on Aunt Esther's ugly black shoes. Just get on with it. Closets aren't part of my contract, little girl."

"Little girl?" I said, wedging my hips between Andy's legs. "Do I look like a little girl to you?" It was a hypothetical question. I knew what he saw when he looked at me—and he looked at me a LOT. For Andy, hanging around was an excuse, not a chore. And protection from a sixteen-year-old was the last thing on my mind.

"I've been watching you," I continued. "You park your Honda outside my bedroom window late at night, when you don't want *Mommy* to see. Three girls in two weeks—wet kisses, your hands under their blouses? I think you're a bad, bad boy."

"Tell me something I don't know," Andy said, "or I'm outta here."

"Wait," I said, putting my hand against his pecs. I could feel his heart racing, a pierced nipple beneath the cloth. "That's not the secret. I just wanted you to know I'd seen you. But, trust me, I totally understand."

"Yeah, right," he said, pulling back from my hand. "Like you'd know anything about that. You've got ten seconds, kid."

Liar, I thought. *You just closed your legs around my hips. You're not going anywhere, until I say go.*

"Ten seconds," I said. "Now, how can I put this?" I pulled my hand back and slipped the tip of my finger inside my mouth, biting softly. My fingers then fell to the open buttons of my garage sale shirt. Andy's gaze went with it. *Good*, I thought. His eyes looked up. I let him see me smile.

"I'm not really a kid," I said in a whisper. "I'm not even a virgin." I let the second half of the statement slip to a nearly inaudible tone.

"Excuse me?" he said, watching my wet finger, now a vague shadow in the valley between my breasts. He leaned closer to hear me, to visually follow the finger. I felt the rhythm of his breath, warm and damp against the side of my face, and leaned past it.

"Men like to touch me," I whispered in his ear, my lips brushing the folds of flesh as I spoke. "It started with this guy my mom was seeing. He was my babysitter, too." I leaned back to see his face. *Yeah*, I thought, *I've got him.* "He made me take a bath, then toweled me off, real gentle like I was blown glass. He loved me, Andy. He said so. He said if I let him kiss me a little, he'd buy me a Malibu Barbie. And I *really* wanted that Barbie." The flashlight beam tilted to one side.

"So you let some fossil kiss you?" Andy pretended he was disgusted. But I could tell by the way he watched my mouth, he wanted to be the guy.

"I did," I said coyly. "Can you guess where he kissed me?" I pressed his free hand against my chest.

"Whoa," he said. "That's twisted." But he didn't try to pull away. If he had any resistance, it melted like a snowball against the flesh cupped in his palm. I pushed into him a little harder.

"You're thinking I'm a liar," I said, as I felt his hand close around my softness. "But it's true—all of it. I swear."

"All girls let guys cop a feel," he said. "Big deal. You've got five seconds."

I ignored him. "The guy couldn't stop thinking about me," I said. "But he wanted me to kiss him back. So the next time we were alone, he bought me a puppy and taught me something new."

"Oh, man," he said, laughing. His legs pulled me closer. "You've still got the dog, so tell me, where did you—"

I interrupted, pressing my mouth against his.

"Baby," he whispered. *Baby*. The magic word, like *victory* flashing neon yellow. It says the game has shifted. Guy, nothing; Wanda, the whole enchilada. Anything else he had to say disappeared with the flashlight on the closet floor. His tongue was in my mouth before I could tell him the guys included my foster dads.

Andy was nobody. The poor jerk had nothing I wanted, other than a car. But messing with him taught me if I made all the moves, I kept all the marbles. I didn't have to wait for some old guy to get an itch. I strung Andy along for rides to school until his *Mommy* caught me going down on him in the backyard. They had me shipped off to a new foster home. So what. They're all the same—boys and foster homes.

Four years and hundreds of dark places later, I could sniff out hormones at a hundred paces. So when poor, heartbroken Johnny Smith tiptoed up to my locker talking about some bogus research project, the scent of sex was obvious.

"You're doing a research project for *psychology* on me?" I said, my inner yellow neon flashing. "Sugar, I think you're doing a research project on me—for *yourself*." I was almost sorry this was going to be so easy. They say nothing lasts forever. I say some things never change.

But here's the kicker. Johnny came clean. He said screwing around on his preppy girlfriends was messing him up and he wanted a shrink to help him stop. He figured I knew plenty of therapists, and maybe I'd share one. No shit. I collected mental health workers like Johnny collected broken hearts. So we struck a deal, but it's not like I hadn't noticed him before.

Johnny was totally doable. Sexy runner's body, dark hair, chocolate eyes. I got antsy just thinking about him, even if he and his ex, Nancy, did cost me my third suspension of the year. Nothing about *that* was my fault. Well, not *really*.

It happened a couple of months ago. "Hey, Johnny," I said during passing period. His locker was, like, two heartbeats from mine. Even in a crowd, he could almost hear me whisper. "Stand still so I can see how much you've grown," I said, pressing my body against him, my hands reaching over his head at his shoulders.

"You're a dwarf, Wanda," he said, laughing. "How are you gonna gauge whether or not I've grown?"

"Five foot two isn't short enough to be a dwarf," I said, smiling, one hand still raised, the other moving gradually south. "If I were a little person," I said as my fingers slid down his abs, "my twins would hit you about here." I was about to flirt with his zipper when I felt an algebra book hit me from behind.

My fingers wrapped around a fistful of jealous girlfriend hair instead of Johnny's package, but it was totally self-defense. Of course, that's not the way Johnny told it. He said I took the first swing. His misguided loyalty cost me three days in bitched-out hell, but it was worth it. Because before she whacked me, Nancy's bad boy was getting wood. And that lock of hair looked great with the Mardi Gras beads on my RAV4's rearview.

Miss "Save It for Marriage" wasn't good for Johnny anyway. I was all for his habit of self-recreation. In fact, imagining

Johnny's hardware pushed me over the edge about a third of the time—when fantasies of Johnny Depp weren't doing the job. But the boy had to be going blind. I figured there was no reason for him to bump it solo when I was primed for the ride.

"So tell me about your mother," I said. "If you want Rita to help, she'll need to know about your mom." That wasn't a lie. My therapist went ape shit whenever I talked about my mother. Go figure. I thought it was the string of "daddies" that got me where I was. But she was the expert.

"My mom is an alcoholic," Johnny admitted, the solar-powered kind that slips into the arms of Jack Daniels when the sun goes down. I never figured Beaver Cleaver's mom for a lush.

"Do your mom and dad sleep together, you know, get naked?" I asked wide-eyed.

"How would I know?" he said, as stunned and insulted as he would have been if I'd planked him with a two-by-four. God, he was so precious. I couldn't resist taking it a step further.

"Does she sleep with you?" That was mean, I know, but he was so easy to mess with. He shot out of his seat like it was drenched in cat pee.

"Your therapist would want to know that?" he said in disbelief.

"Not on the first visit," I said, calmly sipping my chocolate shake. He was about five seconds from a sprint when I eased back.

"Sit down," I said, patting his seat. "Kidding."

He shook his head as he sat down, the blush in his cheeks slowly fading. "Are you going to help me or not?"

"Oh, I'm going to help you," I said, picturing him breathless for a much better reason. "I'm definitely going to show you the way."

I had him eating out of my hand a couple of weeks later. You'd think no one ever listened to him babbling on about how his father ignored his mother and how tough it was to be such a babe. He certainly got that part right. He was incredibly hot. And I was the attentive little friend, complete with visible cleavage and electric "accidents." When my chest brushed his arm as I reached for a menu or my thigh pressed against his when we sat together in a booth, Johnny wanted Wanda Wickham's physical therapy instead of Rita. So I decided it was time to set the hook.

"I can't do this anymore," I said the next time we met. "I mean, what's in this for me? You're getting the chance to build a great relationship. All I'm gonna get is left behind. It hurts to be invisible, Johnny." I worked up a few tears for dramatic effect. "But it's not your fault. You didn't ask me to fall in love."

Ding! Ding! Ding! Johnny's puppy-dog eyes said it all. I'd hit the perfect combination of hurt and lonely. We were horizontal in his father's pickup before he had time to start the engine. That's when things got a little twisted.

I decided to stack on the guilt while I put my bra back on, just like his mommy. "That's okay, Johnny," she'd say. "Run along and play with your friends. I'll just sit alone in the dark until the rum makes me cross-eyed." Should work for me, too.

"Oh, Johnny," I said. "What have I done? I didn't want to do that again unless the guy loved me. And you could never love a girl like me." Then I pumped up a few more tears. But here's the weird part. Once they started, I couldn't make them stop. It was like the floodgates had opened and we were being washed away.

"Well, uh . . ." he stumbled. But I couldn't stop blubbering long enough to listen.

"Don't," I said. "I don't want you to lie." I bolted for my car. For the first time since my eleventh birthday and my second foster father, I couldn't tell what was real.

The waters receded two hours after I drove home and locked myself in my bedroom, but I couldn't stop thinking about Johnny. As he'd peeled my shirt back, it had hit me. This wasn't some old pothead slipping a finger into my *Sesame Street* panties. This was a guy that lied to protect his girlfriend. He was trying to do what was right, even if he didn't have a clue about how to do it. His lips savored every inch of my skin, like a toddler with his first taste of ice cream.

Johnny was the real thing. And I wasn't even a reasonable facsimile. For the first time in my life, that wasn't how I wanted it to be.

For six days, I couldn't look at him without going premenstrual. None of my normal scams—the sassy mouth, the sexual innuendo—got me past it. He'd smile and say he was sorry, and I'd puddle. I'd smell how much he wanted to touch me and hate myself for wanting it too. "That's no way to stay in control," I'd tell myself. But I guess I wasn't listening.

"Meet me at the Frosty Freeze," he said, when I gave up on not answering the phone. "I need to see you."

I told him I didn't trust myself not to touch him, so he promised to be strong enough for us both, but that wasn't what I wanted to hear. I wanted him to lie to me, the way he lied to the girls that really mattered. I wanted him to tell me he loved me so I could hate him when I found out it wasn't true. I wanted the emotional power to play him. But things weren't going my way.

"I'm really sorry," he said, almost before the booth seat was warm. I sat across from him, trying to harness the reach of my legs. I didn't want to accidentally brush against his jock shoes, or his ankle or his leg. That was virgin territory for me—trying NOT to touch a guy that was pressing my buttons.

"It's not your fault," I said. "You don't have to be sorry."

"I'm not sorry for *that*," he said, putting his hand on top of mine. "Touching you was incredible. I liked that. I'm just sorry it made you feel bad. I know you haven't had an easy life."

Another floodgate opened. For the next couple of hours, I did something I never do. I told the truth. He'd seen the best of me, naked and orally fixated in his father's Chevy. Now he'd seen my ugly parts too. He heard about every crack-blurred dealer my mother turned a blind eye to . . . every hand I let touch me after they were through. Every ache and sorrow I'd ever swallowed was on the table. When that was done, panic was all I had left.

"Listen," I said. "I'm gonna drive away now, but I want you to promise me that if something happens, you won't blame yourself."

"Something happens?" Johnny said, worried sick. I hated him for being so sincere. "Something like what?"

"Don't worry about it," I said. "Just promise."

"Something like what?" he said again, more loudly.

"It doesn't matter," I said, feeling the balance starting to return as I slid into my car. "Just know it won't be your fault."

"I do love you, Wanda," he said. "I mean, I think I really do. You haven't been off my mind for five minutes since I saw you last."

I looked up at him, those warm brown eyes full of a tenderness I'd never understand. And for a fleeting moment, I almost believed him. Then I remembered all the dirt I'd unloaded five minutes earlier. *Get serious*, I told myself. *There is no friggin' way.*

I smiled weakly. "You couldn't love me, Johnny," I said, feeling naked to the soul. "Because there's nothing about me good enough to love."

I gunned my engine and nearly ripped Johnny's arm off in the process. If he'd been another guy, burning rubber would have been strictly for show. But being that honest left me feeling uneasy.

Johnny wasn't having it. The guy drove like a NASCAR champion on acid. I tried to lose him. I drove past his house. I drove past mine. But he was relentless. I finally pulled over at the open spot by the river.

The little prick got out of his car and started knocking on my window. *Jesus*, I thought, *doesn't this guy know when he's been thrown clear of a runaway train? What could he possibly want from me now?*

"I do love you, Wanda," he said when I finally rolled down my window. "And I can prove it."

I would have done Johnny Smith that night, even if he'd called me a worthless whore. But I couldn't get enough of him when I let myself pretend we might be in love. I drove home in a daze. I drove home braced for a fall.

It didn't come right away. At first we spent every moment together. Love for Johnny meant driving me to school and helping me cheat in Pre-Calc. Love for me was what happened on the way to school, during lunch, and even every once in a while, during class.

"What in the hell are you doing?" he'd said when I followed him into the boy's room. "Did you miss the sign on the door?"

"There's no mistaking that sign," I said, unbuttoning my sweater. "But what I'm looking for is a man."

Johnny zipped up his fly and bolted in about three seconds flat. Unfortunately, I was still refastening my top when Coach Bob Butler waltzed in for an R-rated view.

"Miss Wickham," he said, "care to explain what you're doing half naked in the boy's restroom?"

"Looking for a real man?" I said, brushing against his PE teacher thighs. "Know any that might be interested?"

"I know one about to give you a Friday detention for being in the wrong bathroom without a pass," he said.

"Oh, come on, Bobby," I said, turning on the charm. "Aren't you getting enough from your born-again wife?"

"Praise the Lord," he said smiling. "I get plenty. And I'll see you for thirty extra minutes this afternoon." He laughed as he pushed me through the swinging door, but I wasn't particularly amused.

Johnny wouldn't talk to me on the way home from school that afternoon. He didn't even want to come in when I told him my foster folks would be gone for at least another hour.

"You don't want me," I said. "I knew it would end. Guys always say they love you, then dump you as soon as you believe it's true."

"We've been over this," he said, his voice laced with frustration. "I want you. But we can't do it ALL the time. I mean a guy runs out of bodily fluids. And no matter how many times I tell you I love you, you never believe it's true. So why should I waste my breath?"

"Because I'm supposed to matter to you," I said, my temper rising. "I suppose you won't answer your cell phone again, either," I continued. "You didn't answer it Wednesday, as I recall. Too busy screwing around with your new girlfriend? Isn't that how we got together in the first place? Poor little Johnny didn't want to blow it with another preppy girl? Except I'm not a preppy, am I, Johnny? I'm just your first stab at dating a whore."

"We're not going to go there today, Wanda," he said. "I just don't have time." He leaned over to kiss me good-bye, but you better believe I turned my face away.

"I don't need you," I said in a panic. "There are plenty of guys who can take care of me if you're not up for the job."

"I'll call you later tonight," he said. "And I'll pick you up tomorrow for school."

"Don't bother," I said. "I could be dead by morning. So pick up your new preppy girlfriend instead."

He wasn't gone five minutes before I was sorry for losing my temper and I remembered I was late for detention with good old Coach Bob. But just as I predicted, Johnny wasn't answering his phone—and I dialed every four minutes to be sure.

"Where are you?" I screamed into the receiver as I put my RAV4 in neutral and walked in fifteen minutes late for a half-hour detention. "You're never there when I need you," I hollered. "I've friggin' had it with you, you worthless little boy."

"Man trouble?" Coach Butler said as I walked into the media center, his feet on the librarian's desk.

"Where are all the other convicts?" I said, throwing my cell phone into my purse.

"No one else was this late, Miss Wickham," he said. "So I gave the others a friendly reprieve."

"Then I'm free to go," I said. "I mean, if the other little hellions were pardoned, shouldn't that apply to me?"

"All the other hellions showed up for detention," Butler said. "So for the next two hours, you're stuck with me."

"Two friggin' hours?" I said. "Jesus, Bobby, won't your little woman miss you when you don't come home for chicken casserole and herbal tea?"

"The little woman is at her five-year college reunion," he said in a husky, sexual tone. "We've got all the time that we need."

Yeah, there was something familiar about all this, something I hadn't noticed since Johnny stepped in to clutter my view. But now that Beaver Cleaver was history, I remembered how broad my options had always been. Coach Bob would do for now, I thought. And at least there was something I could count on. Nothing lasts forever, but when you get right down to it, some things never change.

FALLING DOWN TO SEE THE MOON

by Joseph Bruchac

You don't have to fall down to see the moon.

That's what I thought Sensei Dwight told me right after we bowed out on the foul line. I wasn't happy. It seemed as if our class was over before it began.

The Green Grass Youth Drum was already taking over the gym floor, and there was a lot of noise. It didn't matter one bit to the drum group that they were walking out onto what had been our sacred dojo space only seconds before. Where we had entered on reverent bare feet, they were all now stomping around in muddy sneakers. Well, nearly all of them. I can understand why they have got this multiple-use policy at the Tribal Rec Complex, but I wish the hell they wouldn't schedule things so tightly. I mean the drum group not only has to pile in right after us, some of them even come and sit in the bleachers bored and watching the last part of our class and wishing we'd move our little kung-fu asses out of there.

But, I reminded myself, I had to look at the bigger picture. Just last night I had complained to Gramma Otterlifter about the tight scheduling.

"Every time we start to do something, we have to stop."

She looked up from her fingerweaving and chuckled. "Bobby," she said, "that is probably the idea. It will remind you kids of our heritage. What it has always been like for us Indians to deal with government authority. Be prepared for removal or relocation at a moment's notice."

Maybe that was what Sensei Dwight had meant in that remark. Like that you have to learn from difficulty. He was good at quoting things that made you think. He gave us one of those words of wisdom at the end of every class. It was deep stuff from the ancient masters. People like Kung Fusion or Tao the Ching. I made it a point to remember exactly what he said and then write it down in my notebook as soon as I got home. Here are some of my favorites.

What is the sound of one foot stomping when there is no floor?
It is the hole in the wheel that makes the whirl go around.
You should never slip on the same banana peel twice.
The shape changes, but not the worm.
The tongue is mightier than the bored.
Be a real hole and all things will fall into you.
He who does not trust will be busted.

The other twenty students had already headed for the locker room to get changed. But I was still standing there, thinking about the meaning of Sensei Dwight's latest words of wisdom, as I watched Green Grass set up. Naturally, they had Nancy Whitepath, who was the only one who took her sneakers off, carrying all the chairs. That wasn't fair, but she never complained. Then again, she was the biggest member of the group. Probably the strongest, too. With her size it was a wonder they didn't all just ride on her back. I hadn't thought of it before, but maybe it was just as hard for her being so big as it was for me being so small. Or at least like it used to be for me before I got into martial arts.

The rest of the Green Grassers were acting like they owned the floor, like they had more right to be there than we did. It started to piss me off. Then I shook my head. I had to remember the teachings. Anger makes the wise man act like a fish. Plus, I had the consolation of knowing that Green Grass would have to make an even quicker exit than we did. There was a Lady Warriors basketball game at eight p.m. Of course Nancy would be sticking around, being the star center on the team. She looked over my way, and I made it a point to study my fingernails. Have to keep them short when you're doing martial arts, especially when you are a high belt and need to be a good example to the lower ranks.

"Bobby?"

I looked up. It was Sensei Dwight. I think Sensei was worried that his words of wisdom hadn't reached my discouraged ears. He knows how I tend to drift off. So he said it again, a little louder because of all the noise the drum group was making. They were already deep into practicing one of their Honor Songs. Even above the sound of the drum, you could hear her voice as she stood there, shaking her rattle and singing.

"Bobby, repeat it back to me."

I did, and Sensei Dwight laughed.

"What's wrong?"

"Listen," he said, "I actually may like it better your way. I mean, sometimes you do have to fall down, make a mistake, to learn something. But the saying is a little different than that. It's that you do not have to be TALL to see the moon."

"Oh," I said, feeling my face get red and hoping that Sensei Dwight's deep voice wasn't reaching the ears of any of the Green Grassers. "Cool. I gotta go get dressed now."

After the basketball game, I rode my bike back home alone. It had been a great game. Just like everyone expected, our Lady Warriors had won. Also like everyone expected, she had scored more points than anyone else and also ruled the boards with fourteen rebounds. I'd embarrassed myself only once, being too loud. Even though I'm not the biggest kid around, I've got a voice like nobody else. Sensei Dwight says I can knock people down with my ki-yah when I attack. It was right after she stole the ball and took it the length of the court.

"All right, Whitepath!" I yelled.

A couple people next to me covered their ears, and my best friend, Neddy Coming, dropped his bag of popcorn. The worst part, though, is that she actually turned my way, cocked her finger, and pointed in my direction. Probably telling me to close my piehole. I was down fast and tried to keep my mouth shut for the rest of the game. She wasn't about to forget my idiotic behavior, though. From then on, every time she made a basket she looked in my direction and did that pointing thing. I wanted to crawl under my seat and hide. But it was too good a game to miss, so I just stayed there.

After the game Neddy asked me if I wanted to go with him. Somebody's older cousin was getting them some beer. They were meeting at the lake, and it'd be a blast. I shook my head. I was in training. When you're in training you don't abuse your body with beer or cigarettes or pot. Like Sensei Dwight says, *He who does not know when to stop will find his troubles doubled.*

"Come on," Neddy said. "Maybe your big old girl friend will be there."

I didn't answer that dumb remark. Even your best friends can be jerks. That's not one of Sensei Dwight's sayings. It's just the painful truth. I grabbed my old bike and started pedaling the four miles back home. It was a warm autumn night, and the land around me was so wide and quiet that my mind just started to drift. I tried to steer it away from the game and the way Nancy Whitepath had pointed her finger at me. I thought again about what Gramma Otterlifter said last night about learning from being pushed aside. It was a joke, but there was more to it than that. Like the koans that Sensei Dwight gives us, there's always more there under the surface. Like a fish in clear water. It may look small, but that's just because it's down so deep.

As I thought about that, I found myself wondering what Bruce Lee or someone trained like him would have done during those bad times, back when the Five Civilized Tribes were being forced to leave their homelands by greedy white people who wanted the gold that had been discovered in Georgia. I drifted off into this Hong Kong kung-fu fantasy about the white-haired Evil Master who is behind it all, hiding in his lair while his evil minions destroy the Shaolin Temple and murder the innocent monks. Only this time, the Evil Master is not some old Chinese guy, it's President Andrew Jackson, hiding out in the Hermitage. Even though he is no longer still president at the time of the Trail of Tears, he is still the Hidden Power behind this scheme. But just as he is gloating by the fire, the window smashes and in comes flying not Bruce Lee, but Bobby Wildcat, martial arts master on a mission to restore justice. Bobby Wildcat, a hundred pounds of fighting fury.

The Devil of the Indians is ready, though. Underneath his blanket the Evil Ex-President has two pistols, and he jumps up pointing them at me. He's deadly with those guns. He's killed men in duels.

"Hiiiii-eee-ah!" I leap forward in a perfect spinning back kick and knock both pistols out of his hands.

Oops. Shit! It's not a good idea to close your eyes and do a spinning back kick when you're on a bicycle. The bike and I went off into the ditch.

Fortunately, all my martial arts training served me well. I only got one little bruise on my leg and a torn pant leg. I didn't jump right up. I stayed there on my back looking up at the full moon. It had just risen over the cotton field in front of me. Maybe the fall was worth it to see the moon like that.

My bike, though, wasn't even a white belt. It had never learned how to fall without getting hurt. The front wheel was so bent out of shape that I ended up pushing it the rest of the way home. The only hard part about that was when I heard cars coming and had to get off the road and hide in the bushes so I wouldn't be seen. It was lucky I did because I saw a familiar face in the front seat of the king cab Chevy, the third vehicle that went past. The moonlight reflected off those silver crescent moon earrings she always wears except when she's on the court. She probably doesn't know I made those earrings. When she stopped by my dad's booth at the Indian Arts Fair, she probably figured she was getting something made by Robert Wildcat, famous Indian jeweler, at a bargain price. She sure didn't see me, because I ducked out the back of the tent as soon as I noticed her meandering our way. Of course I had signed those earrings, but the way I sign a piece of silver is the same way my dad does. A wildcat paw with an *R* in the middle. Except I always put in a tiny *2* that most people don't notice. Robert Wildcat II. It always felt nice to see her wear those earrings. Like it made me glad she was in that truck going home with her mom and dad and not headed out to that lake party.

When I woke up the next day, I was stiff all over. It couldn't have been the fall off the bike because I know I ducked my shoulder and rolled perfectly before I hit. It was more likely all the practice I did when I got back home on doing a flying spinning back kick just right. I was out in the backyard for hours jumping and spinning and thumping my heel against the old duffel bag I'd stuffed with rags and hung from the oak tree. I go for my brown belt in six weeks, and I have to get that kick just right. My parents called me in when it got so dark that the bats were flying around me as I practiced, so I don't feel like I've got it yet.

That's what was on my mind as I walked around the corner in the hallway of our school. I was lining it all up mentally. The right position for my arms, the proper breathing, lifting my knees high enough, all of that. And like it sometimes happens when I'm concentrating on something, I closed my eyes. *Whomp*. I walked right into what I thought was a wall. Until it cussed at me and threw me up against the lockers.

"Nosebug, you little shit. You stepped on my foot."

I didn't have to open my eyes to know who said those words. I recognized the sneering voice. It was the person who had given me that despicable nickname back in second grade. I didn't deserve that.

Everybody picks their nose when they're little kids. And that day in Mrs. Bootick's art class, I had brought out a booger that was so black, so round and perfect, that it looked like a little beetle. When it fell off my fingertip and stuck on the paper on my desk, I did what I did automatically, without thinking. I drew six little legs coming out of the booger. I was being creative, just like Mrs. Bootick told us we should be. But Auley Crow Mocker was sitting next to me and saw what I'd done. "Hey," he cawed, "Bobby made a nosebug. Is that your little brother, Bobby?"

Mrs. Bootick snatched my booger beetle paper, crumpled it up, and threw it in the basket. So much for my career as an artist. But not for my nickname.

That was all Auley Crow Mocker called me from then on. Nosebug. Then he beat me up. I tried running, but he would always catch me. I tried fighting, but he just beat me up worse. I couldn't tell my parents. It was too embarrassing.

Neddy, who was my best friend back then, too, tried to make me feel better.

"Just wait," Neddy said. "Auley is a big bully now, but he's probably one of those kids who's only big in grade school. Someone like that used to beat up my dad, but when they got to high school, Dad was twice his size."

The thought that Auley Crow Mocker had gotten his growth too early and would probably turn out to be a pipsqueak was a consolation to me for a few years. Another minor consolation was that beating me up wasn't a big deal to Auley, not like his favorite sport. He just did it whenever he happened to notice me. *He who is not seen does not get hit in this scene.* So, over the next few years, I mostly succeeded—aside from a few bloody noses—in avoiding him. That was good. What wasn't so good was that Neddy was wrong. Auley never stopped growing. We were in high school now, and he was still the biggest bully. He was one of the major reasons I joined Sensei Dwight's karate classes two years ago. One day he'd discover that the little nosebug he'd been picking on all those years had finally turned into a deadly wasp.

But this wasn't the day. I wasn't ready. I didn't even have my brown belt yet. Also, this was not the place. It wasn't the big outdoor ring I'd pictured in my fantasies, like the one where Bruce Lee kicks ass big time in *Return of the Dragon*. It was a school hallway where a teacher could walk out of a classroom any minute. And there'd be one here soon, for sure. Like sharks drawn to blood, a crowd of kids gathered around us. If I got in a fight in the school hallway, I'd get suspended. That was school policy. Anyone caught fighting, even the kid getting the crap beat out of him, was out of school for two weeks. Sometimes it was only the kid who got pulped, since he was left on the floor, his mashed features evidence that he'd been in a brawl, while the one who smashed him slipped away in the crowd of kids. Suspended. That would disappoint everyone, my parents, my gramma, Sensei Dwight.

Especially Sensei Dwight. His words about how learning karate lays a special responsibility on you came back to me like a side kick to the stomach. "Never use your art when you are angry," he said. "The real master of martial arts never looks for a fight. Only use what you have learned when you are in a life-threatening situation or to come to the defense of someone else."

All of which meant that no matter which way I turned, it was going to be the wrong way. It didn't matter whether I tried to fight and got beat up, or ran away from the fight and was called a coward. How could it get worse than this?

But it did. Charlie Wagon, Auley's main henchman, leaned over and stuck his face in mine. "What's the matter, Nosebug?" he said. "You scared uh us?"

Just then, from behind him, I heard a *whoof*. It was the sound someone makes when they take an elbow in the gut. Then there was a *thump* as a body fell on the floor. Charlie turned around and looked up. The only person in school taller than Auley stood looking down at him. Auley wasn't looking back. He was doing a great imitation of a fish out of water flopping for air.

"I am SO sorry," Nancy Whitepath said. She turned to the teacher who stood in the first row of kids surrounding us. "Mr. McReady, I just came around the corner here and accidentally hit poor Auley right in the tummy with my elbow."

She reached down for Auley's arm. "Let me help you up." She yanked, apparently not noticing she was standing on his sleeve. "Ooops!" she said. "I am so clumsy. Now I've torn your shirt."

By now, Auley was crawling away from her large hands.

"Okay, everybody," Mr. McReady said. He held up his hands. "Move on. Nothing to see here."

I may be wrong, but it seemed as if he was trying not to laugh.

I slipped around the corner, wishing I could just vanish from sight permanently. Not only had I not fought back, proving to everyone that I was still nothing but a pathetic little insect, I'd been rescued by a girl. And not just any girl at that, but the one girl I really liked, something I was finally admitting to myself at the moment when I felt like my life was over. There was no way that Nancy Whitepath would ever feel anything more than pity for a wimp like me, right?

MOONING OVER BROKEN STARS

by Cynthia Leitich Smith

I blame the Starbreak Movie Theater for my newfound warrior-princess attitude. No, I don't mean Indian princess, long and leggy, with the flowing black hair à la Malibu Pocahontas. And no, I don't mean the Lady Warriors, that's my b-ball team.

Funny, though, when you think about it, on account of how in the movies, it's always the so-called warrior men who are riding off, painted like clowns, screaming like banshees, and raising Westy wild hell while the women are doing *what*, exactly? Sitting around? Trying to decide what to mush into the blue dumplings or watching reruns of *The Real World: Choctaw Nation*?

Not that we were watching a Western. Nope, it was some martial arts flick with men screaming, "*Aiiieeee!*" and mute girls in kimonos.

"You okay?" my date, Spence, whispered. "If you're bored, we could leave."

I *was* bored, but my mama had raised me with manners. "S'all right," I replied.

I'd said okay to the noon matinee set-up as a favor. Spence was the cousin of my mama's cousins, from the other side of their family. In town visiting. And I hadn't had classes today on account of a teacher-in-service.

Even so, I'd suggested Spence come to my game tonight instead. Seemed safer.

He'd scoffed at girls basketball, and I should've backed out then. But I'd told myself I was being overly sensitive. Next time, I'd trust my instincts.

"You done with this?" I asked.

He glanced at the popcorn. "*Done*, done."

Nodding, I set my empty bag on the sticky floor. As my eyes left the big screen, it dawned on me that, in my place, a real-life Asian girl would probably either be pissed about the movie or laughing her ass off. Or worse, embarrassed someone thought she was really like that. A dressed-up doll. A prop.

Once I straightened in the squeaky velvet chair, Spence apparently decided the flickering dark of Starbreak's mostly empty screening room was handy for more than movie watching—*handy* being the operative word. As in, illegal touching. Grabbed and squeezed. Major foul, especially when I was thinking powerful and righteous womanly thoughts. I'm not sure what happened exactly, how my brain sent the message to my curling fist without checking with me first. One of those reflex things, I guess.

When you're my size, not a lot of boys buzz around. Jogging home after the slap-down at the Starbreak Theater, I fretted that "not a lot" would shrink to none. Bad enough to be Gargantua. Now, I'm Queen Kong. Not that I'm interested in *a lot* of boys, not that I'm interested in a lot of boys buzzing.

But there is this one guy. This squirrelly little guy . . . Billy or Bobby or Robby. The Wildcat. Jittery little thing. He's been watching me for no apparent reason. And the not knowing, it's starting to get on my nerves.

Walking into the Tribal Rec Complex later that day with the rest of Green Grass Youth Drum, it's time to focus, to shake the world off my shoulders, to give the Drum its due. Bobby's there, of course, always is, with the dojo crowd. They're all a little less Bruce Lee, a little more Karate Kid. But the mind-body balance thing, that's cool. I'm into that myself.

"Hey there, Slugger," Tracy said, taking the chair beside mine. "Something on your mind?"

I shook my head and tightened my grip on the rattle. "Someone."

I'm used to singing inside, but I don't like it. It makes me miss the Wind.

Drum practice passed too quickly, always does, and then I was suiting up with my team. Coach said to make this one count, and of course I did what I could. They had solid starters but no depth on the bench, and I was aggressive. It's hard, though, keeping my hands on the ball and my mind on the game.

One of their guards elbowed me in the rib cage—let's pretend it was an accident—as the ball left my hand in a pretty little jump shot. Tricky things, elbows. Often ending up in the wrong place.

The whistle blew. Tie game, and then, seconds later, the whistle blew on another foul.

At the free throw line, every bounce of the ball echoed through the house. I took a deep breath to slow my heart and still my hands. I fought to ignore the swollen knuckles. It's an easy shot; that's why they call it free. Easy, except for the psychology. Their fans were hollering, but I couldn't hear them. I could only hear the ball hit the court.

Thump, thump.

You don't think about it. Thinking will get you in trouble. You don't feel the nerves or the excitement, that won't help either. It's all about trust. Trusting those hours of practice, the thousands of times you shot, the hundreds of free throws in a row at midnight, with nothing at stake, no crowd. All for this moment, breathe, breathe.

Thump, thump. It reminded me of the Drum.

My b-ball danced through my fingertips, rose up to fly—

Whoosh!

"ALL RIGHT, WHITEPATH!" It was like the roar of a dragon, the call of a hero, the geeked-out screech of a fan boy in love. That was it, breaking over the cheering crowd, shimmering and sincere. Mystery solved. And a huge surprise, may I just say.

I pointed and held in my grin.

Gotcha.

It quieted Bobby Wildcat a minute, the first time I pointed his way, and I wondered if I'd misread him. But then he perked back up, adding his cheers to the crowd's.

Together Mama and Daddy spark a pure blazing fire that burns so fierce I always feel warmed up via proximity. My blood's a cocktail made from theirs, the good kind of cocktail, healthy and pure. I don't slouch on account of it.

That night, my folks had been married twenty years, and they'd gone to Lobsterfest to celebrate. He'd wanted to try the pizza. She'd adored the pasta with Alfredo sauce. They'd gone off their diets, guilt-free.

As we settled into the king cab Chevy, I grinned and said, "You didn't have to come back for the game."

"Wouldn't miss it," they replied, both speaking at once, sharing a chuckle. On the road, my folks stole looks and swapped blushes like teenagers.

"About what happened at the theater today," Daddy began as we rounded the turn to our hill. "We'll . . . "

"Pay to get Spence's teeth fixed," Mama finished for him. "Don't worry none."

Daddy chuckled, proud, like they'd already talked about it. His little girl taking up for herself. Kind of thing folks would be jawing on for a while.

It hadn't been funny, though. What with the bruises blooming red and yellow on my fingers, the way they'd made it hard to dribble. Or the way it had made me feel to be grabbed like that. Like I was a mountain and Spence had been trying to get a good firm hold. I didn't know that I wanted to take another chance on a boy in the darkness.

But then Daddy shifted, and Mama grazed his hand with her own, and . . .

Maybe, I thought, *when it works right, two people do become one without either losing anything.* I wondered if Bobby had a girl.

By morning, everybody had heard about my clobbering Spence. Not from me. I hadn't mentioned it at drum practice. Hadn't mentioned it at the game, came straight home after. I was guessing Spence himself hadn't spilled.

So, that left my pal Tracy, who'd gone to yesterday's show, too. The one who'd called me Slugger last night.

The one who called me Slugger when I walked up just now.

"Shouldn't that be Champ?" Joni pitched in.

"Or Victor?" Makayla asked.

"No, wait"—Eddie tends toward the dramatic; spends quality time with her word-a-day calendar—"Warmonger . . . how's that?"

I didn't like it, but the teasing hadn't come from a bad place. Under the jokes, I could read what they meant: "You okay?" "We stand together." "You're our girl."

Last night, Mama called to check on Spence, and his lawyer parents had already whisked him on back to their own oral surgeon in the 'burbs.

He'd be okay, I thought. Self-destructive, self-reconstructive rebuilding is what we all do best. Thinking back on the blood and the screaming and the fact that the theater management asked me not to come back, though, let's just say that maybe I overreacted.

Positive there were plenty of nonviolent means to incapacitate a guy, I swore off my right hook. Whitepath, white stick, peace and negotiation.

Yeah, I decided, give peace a chance.

Wasn't me that Bobby Wildcat was afraid of. I'd figured that out last night at the game, but I had been right that someone in the world made him jittery. It was that Auley Crow Mocker with

Charlie Wagon, of all people, and how could I tell? Well, they were about to wallop on Bobby right there in the high school hall.

Worse, I had a feeling it wouldn't have been the first time.

Now, this was something of a judgment call. After all, I'd sworn to be all dove, to put my rep to rest. But, you know, Auley's no good at negotiations, and Bobby Wildcat's time was running out. Truth was, I didn't have a whole lot of admirers, a whole lot of fans. None to spare anyway. People moved aside for Gargantua. Freshmen, seniors, didn't matter. They cleared the way.

It's the sequel, I thought. *Queen Kong Strikes Again!*

So, I sped down the hall and, just when Auley folded his right into a fist, barreled into him, like I hadn't been paying a lick of attention to where I was going. I had the muscle. I had the size. I had elbows, and I wasn't afraid to use one. He stumbled with a pained "Whoof!" and hit the tile floor.

"I am SO sorry!" I exclaimed. And then I made the kind of noises you do when you're trying to make things better, but did what I could to make them worse. Used my best teacher voice and best teacher smile on Mr. McReady.

Everybody laughed, and Auley and Charlie waved off my fawning, acting the tough guys. No permanent damage, no oral surgery required. Auley was sweet on my cousin Makayla, had a baby with her. I didn't need to worry 'bout those boys messing with me. But they'd forgotten Bobby, at least for now. As for Bobby, he gave me a look that said I had done him no favor.

I wasn't sure why.

After school, Bobby Wildcat found me at the Starbreak Theater in the screening room. I wasn't surprised to see him. Every time I looked up lately, there he was.

I'd snuck in wearing my daddy's Graceland souvenir ball cap backward, hair tucked up, with my letterman's jacket over a Red Earth T-shirt and faded Levi's. I hadn't wanted to press my luck with popcorn or a Coke from the refreshments counter, but Bobby came through with that. Diet and extra butter. Two straws.

"Want some?" he asked.

I did. The show was this vampire flick, all about the penetration.

"Bad movie," Bobby said.

I nodded, reaching up to adjust my right earring. "Awful."

"Love it," he added.

"Me, too." Which was the truth.

Did Bobby mind me saving him from Auley and Charlie? I wondered. Maybe—boys could be like that. Buying into the idea of "the girl" always being the one who needs saving. It was a disappointing thought about the boy into mind-body balance, from a family warm and supportive and substance-free, like mine.

I knew who he was now, remembered last night after saying my prayers. His gramma Otterlifter had found me once when I, maybe two or three years old, disappeared among the cars and trucks at the enormous Walmart parking lot. Carried me, all teary-eyed, to Daddy, who'd been searching, half-crazed with worry. She'd been my hero.

Bobby, he was a year younger, and I'd never paid the juniors much mind. The year difference wasn't such a big deal though. Not when you thought about it. I was friends with juniors on the team.

Bobby had nice, clean hands. One of them bumped against one of mine.

An accident.

I flinched because of the bruises from yesterday, not because I minded.

"You gonna hit me?" he whispered over the wet sounds of disembowelment.

Hadn't even crossed my mind. I asked, "You worried?"

"Nah, but the usher warned me at the door. First I'd heard of it."

So, I hadn't successfully snuck in after all.

"Don't worry," Bobby said. "He promised not to tell."

For a while, we stayed quiet, halfway down the rows, in the middle seats. If I'd judged wrong about Bobby, I'd be grateful for the witnesses. In the squeaky Starbreak chairs, I didn't tower over him. It was nice for a change.

"Thank you," he said, finally getting to the point. "But I could've handled it."

Yeah, right. Was that why he'd come? Because he thought he owed me thanks. Because he thought I'd butted in. It was kind of disappointing. Maybe I'd just been starting to hope for more than that.

"I mean," he went on, "if it hadn't been two against one."

Pride talking, I knew, but he was growing on me. Once I hit the court, I have to watch out for pride myself. Maybe it's worse for boys.

A wolf howled through the speakers, raised its head on screen to the night's luminous glow. It was supposed to be an agent of evil, but I didn't see wolves that way.

"You don't have to fall down to see the moon," Bobby whispered, serious and shy.

Just like that, out of the starry blue. You don't have to fall down to see the moon. I thought about the last time I'd sat in my favorite seat beside a boy. What it must've been like for Bobby having to look over his shoulder all the time. Flexing my punching hand, feeling the pain. It hurts when you fight back, even if somebody else started it.

Then I thought about good times, like last night in the truck with my parents, at the Drum, at the game, right now. And good folks, too. My teasing friends. His gramma.

I felt something then. I'm not sure what you'd call it, but it was righteous, powerful. *You don't have to fall down to see the moon,* I thought, turning the phrase over in my mind. Sounded like fortune cookie bullshit, but . . .

"Sometimes," I said, "you do."

WANT
TO MEET

by James Howe

Max blinks at the computer screen, the cursor blinks back at him. His belly aches. Below his belly aches even more.

> want to meet

Alex sent the words moments ago. No question mark. Just a simple statement of desire. That's what it was: desire. Right?

Max tells himself he's crazy to be getting together with somebody he met online. He's heard all the warnings. But they don't matter now. He wants to meet. He has to. It's a matter of survival. That's what he tells himself, anyway.

> want to meet

> YES! / when?

> the arrowhead, nine, tonight i'll be wearing jeans with a tear above the left knee and a t-shirt that says i am one of the people your mother warned you about

> shoes?

> one on each foot

> what kind?

> max, that is such a weird question / do you have a shoe fetish

> never mind

> don't get testy / we haven't even met / okay, i'll be wearing mocs

> mocs? you don't hunt do you?

> no way. my old man does, though. i hate him / the deer-slayer / should i not wear mocs?

> no, wear whatever you want / you know what i look like, i've told you enough times. still don't get why you've never told me what you look like

> don't want to get hung up on the physical

> why are we getting together then

> down, boy

> sorry. it's just, i feel like we've gotten to know each other, our souls, like, and i can't help wondering what the package for the soul looks like and if maybe we'd want to

> nine, the arrowhead / glad you didn't finish that sentence

> i would have if i hadn't hit send by mistake / nine / i'll be wearing my bunny slippers

> lol. hey, max, i hope i won't disappoint you

> you couldn't

> don't be so sure / just be open okay?
> okay

What was that supposed to mean? What if he *is* one of the people your mother warned you about? What if he's a serial killer who will lure you back to his mirrored, crushed-velvet bedroom for amazing sex and sudden death?

Max shakes the thought out of his head. He is going to meet Alex. Alex.

> funny how we both have x names: me alex, you max
> x-rated?
> x / a sign of the times / our parents' times, when they named us
> x-rated?
> MAX!!!!! you have a one-track mind
> not really. i just / truth?
> please
> i'm lonely is all. i don't know anyone like me / except you

> alex, are you there? say something

> want to meet
> YES! / when?
> the arrowhead, nine, tonight

"Max? Max, where are you going?"
"Out. I'm meeting a friend. I'll be back by eleven."
"Who are you meeting? It's a school night."

"I know that. I'm not new to the planet."

"Don't be fresh. My, don't you look nice."

"Mom, stop."

"Is it a girl?"

"I told you. I'm meeting a friend."

"But you look so nice."

"I can only look nice for a girl?"

"I just meant—"

"Give us a kiss. I'm going to be late."

"Don't be fresh."

In the car, his thoughts fly so fast he gives up trying to catch them. His dad would kill him if he knew where he was going. His mom, well, she might be okay once she got used to the idea. Isn't he her darling baby boy? Still, ever since his brother got married in August, all she can talk about is when is *he* going to meet a girl, he's seventeen and never dated, surely there's *one* girl at Wilson, and what about that nice girl at Michael's wedding, Carly's cousin. Lindsay, wasn't it? She even *called* the next day.

It was so bizarre. Michael had been on this campaign the whole weekend of the wedding to get him and Lindsay together. He'd even pressed some condoms into Max's hand at the reception. *Condoms.* Max didn't know what they were until he looked, and then he about died of embarrassment.

"She's checking you out," Michael had said for the tenth time, arching his eyebrows in the direction of his bride's second cousin. "C'mon, take these. You might get lucky."

My kind of lucky isn't your kind of lucky, Max had thought. It didn't occur to him until the next day to wonder why his brother had been carrying condoms at his own wedding. Heteros were so bizarre. He'd taken the condoms, but he wasn't saving them for Lindsay.

It was a couple of days after the wedding that he met Alex online. They'd been chatting for a month now. He couldn't believe it when Alex told him he lived about ten miles up the road. Funny that they'd never talked about meeting until tonight. They'd talked about everything else—music, movies, school, what they believed in and hoped for and dreamed about, what it was like growing up feeling different and alone. Alex had asked tons of personal questions, but he didn't always answer Max's. Curious but shy, was how he'd described himself to Max. Maybe there *was* something wrong with him. Maybe he *was* a serial killer. Maybe he was middle-aged and greasy. Maybe he was seventeen, like he said, but had the face of a gargoyle. Or maybe he was just ordinary and insecure. Like Max.

Max's fingers trace the outline of the condoms in his pocket as he tries to picture Alex. All that appears on his mental screen is a pornographic version of himself. His brain is set to sex 24/7, but he isn't even sure that's what he wants.

> x-rated?

> down, boy

What *does* he want?

To be calm. That's what he wants. To be calm inside himself. To find a friend.

And maybe—he should be so lucky—to fall in love.

The light changes. A car honks behind him. Max lurches through the intersection and pulls off Route 17 into the parking lot of the Arrowhead Diner before he can change his mind. He kills the ignition, glances at his watch. Four minutes. He'll wait in the car until it's exactly nine, then go in.

He closes his eyes, feels sick and excited. Tonight, at last, he is going to meet another boy who likes boys.

When he walks into the Arrowhead, it is nearly empty, as it usually is at this hour. Not that he hangs out here much. There's another diner that's closer to where he lives. And even though some of the locals eat here, it's mostly a pull-off for travelers, people heading up from the city to get a taste of the country or maybe just passing through. Max has heard stories about rest stops along this road where men get together for sex, one of them not far from here. He thought about going there once, about a year ago, but it made him kind of nauseous to picture it. What did these guys do, anyway, leave their families sitting in the car while they went inside for a quickie? What was wrong with these guys? Maybe homos were as bizarre as heteros. Maybe they all had sex on the brain too much. Maybe we're all sick, Max thinks. Men, he means.

He hates that he thinks like this. Here he is waiting to meet Alex, and all he wants is to feel calm inside and find a friend and maybe fall in love. All he wants is for Alex to be a nice person, somebody with a good face and clean hands, who can talk about what it feels like to be who he is, and won't judge Max for who he is. But who *is* he? A sex-starved nut job. Maybe *he's* one of the people his mother warned him about.

"You need a menu?"

Max looks up. The girl is at most a year older than he is. She's got a baby on the way and no ring on her finger. She looks like she hasn't washed her hair in a week, even though she tries to keep it neat, the few stray strands tucked behind her ears. Max feels sorry for her. He has the ridiculous thought that he wants to put his arms around her and assure her it's going to be okay, even though one look at the lines already growing deep in her face tells you her life is going to be anything but okay.

"Didja need a menu?"

"Sorry. I'm waiting for somebody. I'll just have coffee for now."

She nods. "I'm married," she tells him. "I can't wear a ring because my fingers are all swole up."

Watching her walk away, Max is surprised that she knew what he was thinking. Then he wonders if she tells all her customers the same thing and if she really is married. He imagines she cries every night when she gets home from work.

The door opens and Max's stomach does a flip. A man with a beer belly and a hunting cap walks in, kind of rough looking and mean. *Shit,* Max tells himself, *what if this is Alex?* He reaches for his wallet. He'll leave a dollar on the table and get the hell out of there before the guy can say anything. But then a woman comes in and starts talking to the guy, and the pregnant waitress says *hey* like she knows them, and she seats them at the other end of the diner in the booth next to the stand-up fan and the sign that says *Today's Specials.*

To occupy his mind, Max starts watching the desserts revolving in the display-case, trying to figure out how they make them so tall and what they would taste like if you actually ate them. He thinks they are the most disgusting things he ever saw and wonders why he thinks that, considering that they're somebody's idea of beautiful and a whole lot of people must like them because you see them in just about every diner in the world.

Not that he's been in so many diners. Not that he's been anywhere, really. But he's pretty sure he's right.

The waitress—whose name, Max notices from her tag with the American flag stuck behind it, is Sally—arrives with his coffee. She spills some into the saucer as she puts it down in front of him. Her hands are shaking bad, so he doesn't say anything. He wonders if she has parents and if they're going to help her with the kid when it gets here. He wonders why men are so crazy for sex that they do anything to get it, even make girls pregnant and leave them to work late shifts in diners to pay for Huggies and day-old bread.

"Thank you," Max says, wishing he could give Sally a twenty so she could take the rest of the night off.

"Huh?" says Sally, pushing a strand of hair back behind her ears. "Oh, sure. Let me know if you need anything else."

She is starting to move away when Max hears the door again. He tries looking past the waitress, but can't see anything right away. His hands are like ice.

When Sally goes behind the counter, Max makes out that it's a girl who's entered.

She's small and thin and kind of nervous looking, glancing around like she's there to meet somebody, too. She's got a jacket on, which is odd because it's a hot Indian summer night and the Arrowhead's A.C. isn't exactly up to the job.

Max glances at his watch. It's almost ten after. He figures he's being stood up, and on the one hand he's pissed, but he's relieved, too. Anyway, he can't blame Alex. What they're doing is scary. Maybe next time he'll show. He reaches for his wallet a second time.

"Max?"

He notices the beaded moccasins and the tear in the jeans before raising his eyes. The girl is standing there at the side of the booth.

"Okay if I sit?"

It's not registering. "Um, well, I'm kind of waiting for some-body and . . . how did you know my name?"

"I'm Alex."

She opens her jacket: I'M ONE OF THE PEOPLE YOUR MOTHER WARNED YOU ABOUT.

"You're a girl," he says.

"Does that mean I can't sit down?"

It takes Max a minute to realize his mouth is hanging open. He's probably drooling into his coffee. He doesn't have a clue what to make of this. Alex—his Alex—the guy he's been confiding in for a month, telling his secrets to, even talked dirty to one time, this Alex is a girl.

Finally, he says, "I guess you can sit down." He feels his cheeks burn from embarrassment and confusion.

"Please don't be angry with me, Max," the girl stranger says as she takes off her jacket and slides into the booth opposite him. Glancing at the jacket, she tells him, "I thought I might chicken out when I got here. I didn't want you to know right away it was me."

"The boobs would have been enough of a cover," Max tells her, then says, "I'm sorry. I don't usually talk like that. It's just . . . is your name even Alex?"

"Oh, yeah. Alexis."

"Are you seventeen?"

She bites her lip. "Sixteen."

"Oh, great."

"Next month." She looks at him with puppy-dog eyes and he finds it hard to be mad. It's the embarrassment he feels more than anything. Like, what is she? A girl with a thing for gay boys? A spy checking out the queers online to get all their dirty little secrets, and now what is she going to do? Blackmail him or something? She doesn't look the criminal type. But you never know.

"What are you doing here?" he asks her.

"Duh. Meeting you."

Max is all set to say, "Well, it's been nice meeting you," and leave, but there's something about the girl's face that stops him. Even though it seems like she's the one in charge, she looks even more confused than he feels.

"You want coffee?" he asks her.

She shakes her head, then says, "Do you mind if I eat something? I get hungry when I'm nervous. I mean, real hungry. I could eat a horse."

Max raises his hand to get Sally's attention. "I don't mind," he tells Alex. "I just wish you'd—"

"I don't need a menu," Alex says. "I know what I want. A burger deluxe with onion rings, no fries, and a cherry coke. You hungry? I recommend the fries."

"Why aren't you getting them then?"

"I get them all the time. I live just down the road."

Sally is standing next to them. Max repeats Alex's order and asks for an order of fries for himself.

"So," he says as Sally shuffles away.

"So," Alex says back at him. "Look, I'm really sorry about disappointing you. For what it's worth, I never told you I was a boy."

"Alex, it was a *gay* chat room, okay? I'm a guy. It's a fair assumption that the person I'm talking to in a gay chat room is also a guy."

"I know. I'm sorry, all right?"

Max shakes his head. He should just get up and leave. It's all too weird. He almost feels dirty, like he'd gone to one of those rest stops. *Used*, that's what he feels, but he doesn't know why. He looks over at Alex's hands resting on the place mat in front of her. She has delicate fingers, but the nails have been bitten down to nothing.

"You've got a bad habit there," he says.

"I told you. I get hungry."

"Can't imagine there's much nutritional value in fingernails."

Alex laughs.

"LOL," says Max, and he smiles—not at his own joke but at the sound of Alex's laughter. "I knew you'd have a laugh like that," he tells her.

"You thought I was a boy," she says back.

"Yeah. A boy with a goof-ball laugh."

"Thanks a lot," she says.

"Hey, I like it. Honest."

They return their gaze to the table, staring at their own hands for a time, fiddling with their napkins and silverware, waiting for the food to come. He starts to speak, but then figures he may as well let her do the talking. This is her game, after all; she's the one with the rulebook.

"I needed to see you with my eyes," she says at last.

"As opposed to, what? Your nose?"

She doesn't laugh this time. "As opposed to my imagination. I needed to know you were real."

Max looks up from the table and into Alex's eyes. He tries to connect the person across from him to the person he's been talking to every night for weeks. That person started feeling like his best friend; this person is a total stranger.

"So how real are *you*?" he asks at last. "I still don't get it, okay? Were you looking for a boyfriend? I mean, talk about looking for love in all the wrong places."

"I wasn't looking for a boyfriend," Alex says, blushing. "I was looking for answers."

"Did you find them?"

Alex bites her lip again. Max thinks, *definite oral fixation.* But then he thinks what courage it must have taken for her to come here tonight.

"How'd you get here, anyway?" he says as Sally puts their food in front of them, her hands still unsteady as she asks, "Can I get you guys anything else?"

He tells her no thanks, and Sally moves slowly, dreamily away.

In the distance, the man with the hunting cap has folded his arms over his belly. He stares right through the woman across from him as if she isn't there. The woman has her head turned toward the window. Even from where he sits, Max can make out her unblinking eyes looking vacantly back at her.

Alex slathers her burger with ketchup, takes a bite the size of all outdoors, and says, "Rode my bike."

"You rode your bike? There are crazy drivers on this road at night. You got reflectors?"

"I come here all the time," Alex reminds him, mid-bite. "Anyway, I got reflectors. And don't worry, Mom. I got a helmet, too."

Max's stomach takes a little turn. The way she says that sounds just like the Alex he knows, the one he *thought* he was meeting.

"So did you get the answers you needed?" he asks again.

Her mouth full, she nods. "All except seeing you," she says when she can speak. "I mean, you could've been anybody. A mass murderer or that guy over there with his hairy beer gut sticking out because he can't even get his shirt to stay down. Ugh, that is so gross. Or—"

"Or a girl."

Alex blushes for a second time. "But you're not any of those things. You're the same nice guy you seemed like online. And that's what I needed to know. I've got my reasons."

"Which I have the feeling you are not going to share with me. Why is that, if you don't mind my asking?"

Alex puts down her burger and takes a long swig of her cherry coke. She turns her head and stares at the man in the far booth.

Turning back, she goes, "That guy over there?"

Max nods.

"He looks a lot like my dad. I wasn't kidding when I told you I hate him. My old man, I mean. He's a bully son of-a-bitch, and I wish he'd drop dead. I'd kill him myself if I could figure out how to get away with it."

Max starts to object, but Alex doesn't let him.

"How would you like it if you had a father who was drunk half the time and called his own daughter a piece of ass, who treated his wife like she was his slave and his whore? How would you feel if you were the son of a father like that?"

"I wouldn't like it," Max says.

"Wouldn't like it?"

"I'd hate it."

"Yeah, faggot, you'd hate it, all right."

"Hey!"

"That's what he'd call you. He'd call you faggot and pussy and piece of shit. He'd tell you that you had arms like a girl's and he could snap 'em in two if he had a mind to. He'd make you go hunting and fishing and play football and other stuff you don't like and aren't any good at, and if you didn't do them, he'd use you for his personal punching bag."

Alex's hands have turned into fists. Her meal sits half-eaten, forgotten. She stares at the man across the diner until finally he turns and scowls at her, and she looks away, back at Max, who doesn't know what to say.

"My house is like a prison," she tells him, "and my dad is the warden. Maybe I just needed to find somebody nice to talk to. Maybe that's what I was looking for along with answers."

She picks up an onion ring, then puts it back down on her plate. "They get cold fast," she says. "Listen, Max, I'm sorry I messed with your mind, and I'm sorry if I ruined this big evening you had planned."

It's Max's turn to blush. "All I wanted was to meet you," he says. "Or to meet the guy I thought was you."

"Maybe you still will."

"Huh?"

"Who knows? It could happen. I better go," she says, nervous all of a sudden. She reaches into her pocket and pulls out a few wrinkled ones.

"I'll get it," Max tells her.

Ignoring him, she drops the money on the table. "Really, I better get back. He's out with Ray tonight. He never gets home before eleven, but it would be just my luck . . ."

"Do you want to talk—online, I mean?"

"I don't know. Maybe. I don't know." She leans across the table and kisses Max lightly on the cheek. "You're just who I hoped you would be."

"What does that mean?"

"It means, thank you for caring that I have reflectors on my bike."

She looks back at him from the door of the diner, bumping into Sally as she turns. Sally's hand moves protectively to her own belly. *Maybe she is married,* Max thinks, hoping that if she is, it isn't to somebody like Alex's father.

The man in the hunting cap snaps his fingers. "Sally!" he calls out. "How about a check, huh?"

The woman sitting opposite him continues to stare out the window, her reflection staring back at her like a ghost.

Max doesn't hear from Alex again. She's no longer a regular in the chat room, and when he tries to e-mail her, his e-mails come back, undeliverable. He doesn't know her last name or where exactly she lives. He has to laugh when he thinks of all the information she got out of him, even his phone number, and how little she told him about herself. Half of what she did tell was lies, stories about a boy named Alex.

Max gives up on the chat rooms, goes back to being lonely.

Then one night a few weeks later, the phone rings. It is someone named Cal asking for Max.

"My sister told me I should call you," he says. "She wouldn't tell me how you met, but she sure knows a lot about you. She says we have a lot in common and we should get together. I don't know, I mean, do you want to?"

"Meet?"

"Yeah."

"Great."

"Do you know the Arrowhead Diner?"

"Who doesn't?" Max says. "They're famous for their fries."

Cal laughs. Max gets a chill from the sound of it. He swears he's heard that laugh before.

And, of course, in a way, he has.

MEETING
FOR REAL

by Ellen Wittlinger

Alex pulled the curtain shut over the door to her room, as if a thin piece of cloth was enough to keep out the sound of her brothers' arguing. Why, she wondered, didn't Cal give it up? He'd never get James to change his mind anyway. Discussing it just gave James an excuse to act mad and mean, the personality he'd inherited from their dad and was beginning to enjoy.

"I don't understand how you can treat anybody like that, much less somebody you once loved," Cal said as he broke eggs into a bowl on the table.

"I never said I loved her! Jesus, Cal, you sound like Mom used to—everything is supposed to be a big romance. I slept with her, that's all. There was no *love* involved."

"I don't think she'd say that."

"I don't give a rat's ass what she'd say!" James peered into the bowl. "If you're making eggs again, at least put some bacon or ham or something in them. I'm sick of those faggy *omelets* with a few strings of mozzarella cheese."

"I'm frying bacon on the side," Cal said, and to prove it, took a huge slab of pork fat out of the fridge. "Alex, can you come out here and make some salads?" he called to the curtain.

Alex sighed and put down the book she hadn't been reading anyway, but she didn't get up immediately.

gotta go, she typed into the computer.

ok, **Max answered.** can you talk later tonight?

> i think so. 8:30?

> i'll be here.

Alex wished this was one of the nights James had to work and her dad wasn't expected home until late. Those nights she and Cal could have real conversations at dinnertime, about important things. Sometimes they even talked about their mother and where they thought she might be.

James was stalking around the kitchen, pounding his fist on the countertops. "You just don't get it, Cal. This is the kind of trick women pull on guys all the time. They get themselves pregnant and then they expect you to marry 'em. Well, I've got a surprise for *her*."

"Oh, she got *herself* pregnant. I didn't realize that," Cal said. James glared at him.

Alex heard the truck pull into the backyard and came barreling through the curtain. "Shut up! Dad's home!"

"I don't care if he is," James said, but he sat down at the

kitchen table and bent his head over his textbook. He was learning to be an electrician, slowly.

Alex rummaged through the refrigerator and came up with half a head of lettuce and a red onion. "Is this all we have? No tomatoes or anything?"

Cal shook his head. "The good ones are done for the season."

"I don't want that rabbit food anyway," James said, just as the door banged open, letting in a warm breeze and Jim Bellarose, his face flushed already from the two hours of drinking he'd managed to squeeze in since leaving the factory.

"Who's having rabbit food? Not me. I want a piece of meat for a change. Doesn't anybody in this house know how to cook a piece of meat?"

In fact, none of them did. Since Jim's wife, Cindy, had run off the year before—"disappeared like a thief" was how he put it—they'd eaten mostly what Cal figured out how to make. He didn't mind the cooking, only the complaining.

"What's wrong with you, missy?" Jim looked at his only daughter. "You're old enough to be learning how to cook a goddamn meal around here once in a while. It's a woman's job, I don't care what anybody says. Men who cook are queer as a three-dollar bill," he said, staring into the bowl of eggs and milk Cal was mixing up.

"That's an old-fashioned idea, Dad," Alex said. "I mean, lots of guys—"

"Are you talking back to me? You are a big know-it-all, missy, and that's why you ain't ever gonna get a man interested in you." He poked his finger into her back and ground it in hard. "Even boys your age don't want that back talk. You hear me?" He ground harder. "*You hear me?*"

Alex hated having to agree with him on anything, but she knew he'd poke her and hound her all evening if she didn't give in. "Yes, I *hear* you, Dad. I hear you."

"No man's gonna want you, and no woman's gonna want this here pansy of a brother of yours. I'll be stuck with the both a yous the rest of my damn life."

Oh, no you won't, Alex thought. *Not if I can help it.*

James snickered, and their father stalked off to his bedroom to pull off his steel-toed boots. Cal and Alex communicated with their eyes, as they always had around the other two. They told each other *I'm sorry* and *He's crazy*, the way they'd learned from their mother.

Cal sometimes talked to Alex about being gay, but she didn't really understand all of it. Oh, she understood that her brother was attracted to men and not to women, but she didn't really appreciate how that affected him day to day. Nor did she understand why some people hated homosexuals and called them stupid, insulting names. Her brother Cal was the nicest person Alex knew, and probably the smartest person too. Most people seemed to like Cal, even though he kept to himself after school and never hung around with the other seniors like he could have. He told her once that they were nice to him *because* he didn't try to hang with them, but she didn't want to believe that.

When Alex first found the gay chat room online, she only intended to "listen" in, not chat with anybody. She wanted to know if other gay people were like Cal, picked on and kind of lonely. She wondered if there were other teenage boys who would understand her brother's problems better than she could. Maybe she could get some ideas from them about how they coped with a miserable father who called them things like *pansy* and *faggot*.

The talk was fascinating. Yes, people did talk about their parents, but also about the girls they pretended to like, the boys they had crushes on, the teachers who helped them and the ones who sneered, the friends who supported them and the ones who acted like they had the plague, their sex lives or lack thereof, and what they hoped might happen to them in the future. For the younger people, the future was everything. It offered the enormous hope that they could stop pretending to be somebody they weren't. Sometimes it meant they'd be old enough to run away from the people who were tormenting them. And almost always it meant their life could finally, really begin.

The more she logged into the chat room, the more Alex began to understand how Cal felt. Strangely, she began to feel that she really knew some of these people, though she'd only heard them "talk" online. One boy in particular, Max, caught her attention. Often he said something that reminded her of Cal, and she started thinking how much the two of them would like each other. Finally, one evening, she responded to something Max wrote. When she signed herself *Alex*, she wasn't even thinking about fooling him, but when he wrote her back and asked if she wanted to go into a private chat room with him, it was obvious he thought she was male. Alex didn't correct this mistake. At first, she was embarrassed about lying to Max, but then she decided she was doing it for Cal and that made it okay.

Within a few weeks, Max and Alex were discussing everything—their parents, their schools, their friends, their need to talk to someone like themselves. Alex found she could make jokes with Max and he *got* them. He was funny too, and kind, it seemed. He was the closest thing to a best friend she'd ever had. Or rather, he was the closest thing to a best friend *Cal* had ever had. Because most of the time Alex answered the questions as if she *were* Cal. But sometimes she forgot who she was supposed to be and answered as herself. Max didn't seem to notice, but sometimes Alex got so confused about who she was and who she was talking to—her brother? her boyfriend? her brother's best friend?—that she'd tell Max she had to study and get off the computer.

When it turned out that Max lived ten miles away from her, Alex got nervous. What would happen now? If he wanted to meet her—well, he wouldn't want to meet *her*. She would have to figure something out. Maybe she would have to tell Cal. But not yet. Not yet.

"Hey, I stopped by the Arrowhead after work," Jim Bellarose said as he ripped chicken meat from a crispy leg. Cal had gone to KFC and brought home a barrel of chicken and a tub of mashed potatoes just so he wouldn't have to listen to the complaining for one night.

James was stuffing potatoes into his mouth but looked up at his father. "Yeah?"

"Yeah. Saw your little knocked-up girlfriend. She's not looking so pretty these days with that big belly on her."

James shrugged. "Her own damn fault. I thought she was on the pill."

"Did she tell you that?" Cal asked.

"I never asked her, smart-ass. I assumed anybody who wasn't stupid as dog crap would automatically be taking it."

"You can't count on women," Jim Bellarose growled. "You can never count on 'em."

Alex stirred the gravy around in the middle of her mashed potatoes until she'd made a swamp. She'd always liked Sally, but now Sally wouldn't even speak to her. She hated the whole family, and who could blame her?

James rifled through the chicken barrel until he found a fat breast. "We should have this every night. This is a whole lot better than the junk Cal makes."

Cal wiped his fingers on a napkin and stood up, taking his plate to the sink. "Thanks a lot. I'm the only one around here who even *thinks* about feeding anybody else but himself."

Jim laughed. "Oh, now you hurt his feelings, Jamie. He's gonna cry. Boo-hoo!"

James snorted. "He gets his feelings hurt every five minutes."

When Cal walked out of the room, Alex got up too, her plate swimming in gloppy potatoes.

"Where you going, missy?" her father said. "You left a pile of food on that plate."

"I'm not hungry," she said.

"Give it to me," James said, and grabbed the plate out of her hand.

"You running back to your room to play with that expensive toy your mother talked me into buying you? Every night, that's all you do is bang around on that computer. Where you think that's gonna get you, huh? Not gonna get you a boyfriend, that's for sure. Boys don't want some smarty-pants who thinks she's too good for 'em."

"Some boys like smart girls," Alex said.

"No, they don't," James said, as though he were the final authority on the matter. "They just pretend to so they can get laid once in a while."

But Jim Bellarose didn't laugh. He was staring at Alex now. "You're not a *bad*-looking girl, really. Not a bad piece of ass at all. Your problem is, you just can't keep from running your mouth. Just like your mother."

Every time the words *your mother* came out of Jim Bellarose's big mouth, it made Alex want to cry. She missed her so much. How could she have left Alex here with her father and James? Of course, Alex had Cal. Maybe that's what her mother had been thinking—that the two of them could save each other.

Alex took her milk glass to the sink and began to run hot water for the dishes. She *would* save Cal, if she could, and then maybe he'd save her too.

"What happened to that tall hippie kid you were hanging around with for a while? Cory somebody?" James asked. "Did he have the hots for you, or something?"

"Cody," Alex said. "Cody Marker. I was helping him with math." She plunged her arms into the hot water and shivered as it heated her all the way up her spine. She had wondered herself if Cody's interest in her might have to do with something other than schoolwork, but it hadn't panned out that way. It never did. Once Kendra Graham started flirting with him, he didn't seem so interested in Alex's ability to explain geometry.

"Math!" James practically choked. "The way to a man's heart is through arithmetic! That's a new one!"

Jim Bellarose shook his head. "I tell you. How old are you, Alex? Sixteen? I had half a dozen girlfriends by that age. You better not turn out an old maid."

"I'm not sixteen until next month," Alex said.

"Oh, right," Jim said. "We're planning a big surprise birthday party, aren't we, Jamie?" He reached across the table to poke his son's biceps. "Where we invite a buncha really horny *boys*!"

The two of them laughed like fools.

Alex said nothing. She finished the dishes, walked behind the curtain, and signed into the chat room. There was Max.

want to meet, she typed. Sure, it was risky, downright scary, actually, but what other choice was there? She had to see him, to know he was real, to know there was somebody out there who was different from her father and James. Somebody who was like her. Like her and Cal.

As she rode her bike along the highway to the Arrowhead, she was wishing there had been someplace else close by for them to meet. Her dad had said Sally was working tonight; it would be awkward if they didn't speak to each other. But she hadn't wanted to ask Cal for a ride. He would have had too many questions.

Max had said "YES!" as soon as she asked about meeting him. He'd been wanting to, obviously. Was he nervous too? He couldn't possibly be as scared as she was. What if he wasn't who he said he was, either? What if he was a big jerk? Or an old guy? Or a . . . girl? That would be something, wouldn't it? Or what if he just didn't show up at all? Which would be worse? She had no idea, but she slowed down so as not to get there first.

She breathed deeply and threw open the diner door. It didn't take more than a brief glance around the room to find him. He looked just the way he'd described himself: raggedy blond hair, rimless glasses, skin too pale for the end of a hot summer. And very nervous.

She walked to the table. "Max?" He stared up at her, not figuring it out, of course, even after she opened her coat and showed him the shirt that said I'M ONE OF THE PEOPLE YOUR MOTHER WARNED YOU ABOUT. "I'm Alex," she said.

She'd never seen anybody look so thrown for a loop, and it made her feel lousy. Max was obviously very disappointed. He wouldn't have been disappointed if Cal had come. He was expecting Cal.

There were some awkward moments as she sat down across from him and answered his questions. Yes, her name was Alex— Alexis, really. No, she wasn't seventeen (although Cal was), but she was almost sixteen. He kept staring at her as if the answer to the *big* question would be written on her face somewhere. Finally she told him she was hungry, which was suddenly true. She wanted to eat something that wasn't chicken poisoned by cruelty.

When he motioned Sally over to order their food, Alex glanced up at her, but Sally pretended not to know who she was. *It's not my fault*, she wanted to tell Sally, but instead she put her index finger into her mouth and ripped off what little nail there was left.

It was weird. He wanted to know why she—a girl—was there. But she didn't exactly *know* why. She just wanted to talk to him. She didn't know what to say, although she yakked on anyway. Like her dad said, she couldn't keep her mouth shut. Finally Max made a joke about her fingernails. It wasn't that hysterical a joke, but she was so on edge, she laughed loudly. A big idiotic guffaw.

"LOL," Max said. "I knew you'd have a laugh like that."

"Except you thought I'd be a boy," Alex said.

"Yeah. A boy with a goofball laugh."

"Thanks a lot," she said, but it made her happy that she'd pleased him. That she was, in some small way, who he'd expected.

"Hey, I like it," Max said. "Honest."

He *was* honest—she could tell. He would never have deceived her the way she'd deceived him. He deserved an explanation, and she tried a few out before she finally told him the one that seemed closest to the truth.

"I needed to see you with my eyes," she said. "To see if you were real."

It was all she could tell him just then. Over her burger and onion rings they talked more, and it became easier. He began to seem almost like her best friend again, a best friend who was also a stranger.

She told him about her father, about how much she hated him and how badly she wanted to escape. But she didn't mention Cal, didn't say a word about the person who should have been there instead of her. She thought about Cal, but then pushed him out of her mind. She wanted it to just be her sitting there with Max. She wanted his pale blue eyes focused only on her.

Of course, she couldn't have that, not really. Cal could have had it, but she couldn't. The onion rings she usually loved suddenly tasted like garbage, and she wanted to leave. She made an excuse about having to get home before her father got back, as if he'd be sober enough to know whether she was home or not.

"Do you want to talk—online, I mean?" Max asked as Alex gathered her jacket and paid her bill.

"I don't know. Maybe. I don't know."

I don't know one thing, is what Alex was thinking. *I'm an idiot, and I don't know one thing*. And then, before she could think what she was doing, she leaned across the table and gave Max a kiss on the cheek. She was pretty sure it was a kiss good-bye.

As Alex turned to leave, there was Sally, right in the doorway, and she ran smack into her. Sally's hand went immediately to her stomach, as though she was already protecting the baby inside, Alex's *niece*, she thought now, the baby her brother wanted nothing to do with.

Alex wished she could put her own hand on Sally's bulging belly, could help soothe the child that was barely wanted. But Sally backed away and then was gone. *If only I knew what was the right thing to do,* Alex thought, *I would do it.*

A few weeks later, Cal came home from school with news of interest to Alex. He was glad to have something good to tell her; she'd been very moody and depressed lately.

He pretended to knock on her curtain, then stuck his head around it. "Hey, guess what?"

"What?" Alex was sitting in her computer chair, but staring out the window, as usual these days. She'd hardly used her computer in weeks, and hadn't gone into any chat rooms since her evening with Max at the Arrowhead. It was easier to think he might be missing her too than to admit that she wasn't the friend he had in mind.

Cal came in and sat down on her bed. "I was in the library after school, and this guy came up to me and asked if I was your brother, and I admitted that, unfortunately, I was."

She didn't laugh. "Who?" she said, without interest.

"Cody Marker."

Alex's head swiveled from the window to her brother. "Cody Marker? Why did he want to know if you were my brother?"

"He asked me if you were okay. He thought you seemed upset about something."

She turned away again. "I hardly know Cody Marker."

"That's not what it sounded like. I got the distinct impression he was interested in you, dearie. He told me you had the best laugh he'd ever heard. Except that he hadn't heard it in a while. Which is why he thought you were upset. Personally, I think the guy is on to something."

"Cody said that? For real?"

Cal nodded and smiled. "For real. I told him I thought you'd appreciate it if he called you this evening. See how you were doing. I have a feeling he will."

Instead of the happiness he expected to see take over Alex's face, her bubble of sadness burst into wet tears.

"I thought you liked Cody?" Cal said.

Alex came over to sit next to Cal on the bed. "I do. I'm just such a stupid, selfish jerk." She cried all over his shirtsleeve.

He put his arm around her shoulder. "What is going on with you, Alex? I'm starting to get worried."

She reached for a tissue on the night table and wiped her face. "I'm sorry, Cal. It's just . . . I was so lonely. You know?"

"Of course I do," Cal said. "We live here in the jungle with the beasts. I don't know why you're apologizing to me—"

"Wait!" Alex said, leaping up. "I have something for you too. I know this will sound kind of crazy, but I met this guy, a gay guy." She began to rummage through her desk drawer. "He's your age and he's really nice and I know you'd like him, and—"

"What? What gay guy? How did you meet—"

"Never mind about that. I'll tell you later, or he can tell you. But you absolutely *have* to call him. He only lives about ten miles from here." Finally she pulled a scrap of paper from the desk. "Here! Here's his phone number!"

"Alex, I can't call somebody I've never even met!"

"I met him *for* you, and I'm telling you, he's great. Promise me you'll call him?"

It took Cal a few days to get up the nerve to call the number. Alex—who was in a much better mood now that Cody Marker had phoned several nights in a row—kept after him. She told him everything she knew about Max (except how she'd met him) and made him sound wonderful. Cal was worried. He'd never met another gay person his age. He wouldn't know how to act, what to say. He was afraid he'd sound naive.

"That doesn't matter. Just *call* him," Alex said, and finally he did.

"My sister told me I should call you," he said, feeling ridiculous.

But Max sounded just as nice as Alex had said he'd be, and after talking for a few minutes, they made a plan to meet at the Arrowhead Diner.

"I should tell you what I look like," Cal said.

"You don't need to," Max said. "I'll recognize you by your laugh."

NO CLUE, AKA SEAN

by Rita Williams-Garcia

What a bug-out. Here I am watching you pretending not to watch me. I'm not turned off by shy, but shy will get you sitting by your lonesome. Shy will get you watching from the sidelines while I'm stepping out with some other guy. Come on, Sean. Let's get in the game. Say those two words as only you can say them: *Hey, Raffina.*

I have to admit the whole shy thing is part of the appeal. Sean's a complete switch from what I'm used to dealing with. A girl can't eat a hoagie in the caf without some playa rolling up, trying to get those digits. Now that's a turnoff. Guys assuming too much, too soon. It's not just because I'm fine—which I am, but because I'm Gary's sister. The Highlander Hero. Holds the state record for the most triple doubles in a season. Scores thirty-two points on a slow day. So you know what that means. Everybody's scouting. Recruiting. Rubbing up on him, trying to get to know him. Yeah. Even if they have to go through me to be in with Gary. The guys want to be part of the entourage. The chicks want to be the girl in the prom picture when ESPN takes a look back on the life of Gary Frazier.

But Sean? That boy has no clue. He just gives me that smile like he wants to kick it, but swallows it instead. Except when he wears his University of North Carolina jersey. I bet he thinks it's just a cool shirt. Baby blue to play off his blue eyes. Never even seen Vince Carter charge and dunk for the Tar Heels wearing number 15. But I'm not complaining, because when he wears the lucky blue jersey I get those two words from him, "Hey Raffina." Then he'll ask a question, just to have something to say.

And I'm like, *yeeeaah*. Sounds silly. All these guys trying to get me in their Jeep, their Lexus, but I'd rather ride off with Sean in his beat-up hooptie, because he knows how to say my name. It's my parents' fault. Back in the day, Daddy took Ma to see some play about South Africa called *Sarafina!* Yeah. One *f*. After that Ma wanted to name me Sarafina but she couldn't exactly remember the name or how to spell it. So with Daddy's help I got no *Sa* and two *f*s. Because of that people say "raff," like drop my name in a hat, shake it up, and reach for a raff. Why? Because that's what you do when two *f*s are stuck together. Only family gets it right. Family and Sean.

Sean is cool without effort. You know how hard that is? He's not trying to be a surfer, a skater, a prep, a goth, a punk. He's just Sean. A John Mayer cute white guy without the acoustic guitar. When he does finally get it together, he's not gonna say, "'Sup, yo?" changing his style because he's talking to me. He's just going to be real. Sean. With No Clue, he's got all this good stuff going on.

It should be simple. I don't exactly bite. Here we are, two humans taking Human Relations 2. Come on, Sean. Let's relate.

Today's class is all about the female genitalia, breaking it down to the labia minor, major, clitoris, urethra, vagina. It's not exactly helping the cause. Sean won't even look this way. His eyes are straight on the board. Thanks, Mr. Adams. Guess I gotta wait for lucky blue jersey day. Sean's wearing green checks. Green checks? I swear. White boys dress like they're in the third grade. But that's all right, Sean. I'm gonna hook you up. Why? Because you're taking me to the junior formal. You don't know it yet. Just wear the lucky jersey tomorrow and say, "Hey Raffina." I'll do the rest.

I still have to break it to Gary that I'm going out with Sean. (And to Sean too, for that matter.) Gary thinks he has to approve of my boyfriends. He really shouldn't care that Sean's white. I mean, Gary deals with a lot of white girls. Gary's into long hair. Real long hair. No weaves, no extensions.

I'm not like that about Sean. I won't lie. I love his blue eyes, and even that mole on his neck. But that's not why I'm going out with him. And no, I don't want blue contacts. I just like the whole Sean package. And he'll be even better when I get through with him.

I laugh to myself. Gary's gonna have a kitten. And don't let him see Sean rocking that Vince Carter joint. He might as well be wearing Michael Jordan's jersey. UNC is the only school my brother's considering. He visited some other schools. Syracuse. Too cold. UCLA and Gonzaga. Too far. Kentucky. A possibility. But he only wants North Carolina. He only wants to be a Tar Heel. Even ordered a jersey, sweatband, and socks online. He doesn't wear any of it. Doesn't want to jinx himself. Just keeps the stuff wrapped up in plastic. Got it hanging over his dresser mirror like it's a museum display. If I wanted to piss him off, I'd rip open the plastic and touch all his NC stuff with my bare hands.

I just confront him in the kitchen.

"You know I'm going to the junior formal, right? You know I'm not going alone."

"Oh, yeah?"

"Yeah."

Gary palms the top of my head with his King Kong hand. His finger's too close to my eye. I take a swipe at him, but his body is too far from his hand. "Lank-ass ape. Get offa my hair. Ain't no basketball."

"Sister head," he says, sporting his Shaquille O'Neal endorsement grin. "Perfect for dunking."

"Maaaaaw," I holler.

"Rescue who?" Gary says. "I'm buying Ma a bigger house." Then he lets up. Totally wrecked my wrap. Know how long it takes to swirl it and pin it with every strand in place? See, Sean would never do that. I'd get nothing but respect from Sean.

Gary thinks he's my daddy. He thinks he's the man of the house. Well, technically he is, but that don't give him the right to mess up my hair.

"Why you can't wait to get with these losers?"

"Here we go," I say.

"You don't know guys like I do, Raffina. If you did, you wouldn't let one cough on you."

"And how many girls you go out with this year, Gary? Oops. I said go out. That means you'd actually have to go somewhere with them. As in take them out on a date."

"I go out."

"No, Gary. You go *in*."

He laughs it off but he knows it's true. Gary has girls hiding in his locker. Gonna give him some in the weight room, under the bleachers, in the parking lot.

"All right," he says, trying to be serious. "What's so good about this guy? Why he gotta date my baby sister?"

I'm tired of that baby sister crap. That's why Gary runs it into the ground. To annoy me. Just a few years ago we were the same height. Now Gary's six-seven and growing.

I almost say Sean's name, but I can't because everything's not in place yet. I say, "He knows how to treat a girl. That's all you need to know for now."

Gary goes back to being my daddy. "If you're going to this junior formal, I better see this Nigro. You got me?"

I almost laugh. He just assumes who I'm going out with. But Gary's Mr. Equal Opportunity. White girls, Hispanic girls, some black girls. As long as they have long hair.

I don't answer, because Gary's not my daddy. His King Kong hand goes for my head.

I get to class ahead of Sean, hoping today is the day. Sure enough Sean comes in. Baby blue North Carolina Tar Heels number 15 lucky ass shirt. I'm smiling, feeling these lips on those lips. Come on, Sean. Say the two magic words, and I'll do the rest.

I'm still waiting for the turn. The grin. The "Hey, Raffina." But nothing. Dag on, Sean. What's the problem? We're sitting in the sex class. The teacher's showing pictures, talking about organs engorging. I see you trying to sneak a peek. Come on, Sean. I'm not wearing these low-cut V's for nothing. At least give me some energy. The famous Sean grin.

I'm starting to doubt myself. I can't tell if it's because he's shy or what. Then I look at him. Sean. Clueless Sean. Then it hits me. *Duh!* Girl, you're so stupid. He's never kicked it to a black girl. This is probably a big thing to him. Here I am planning how I'll dress him for the junior formal, while he's going over the whole black and white thing, like Hamlet and whatnot. To kick it or not to kick it.

Damn. I thought that stuff was back in the twentieth century. Nobody's going to stare at us. Maybe Sean's got a reason to be freaking. Like, "Raffina, I have to tell you something. My family was on the *Oprah* show. You know the episode. 'My Father Is a Grand Wizard of the Local KKK.'"

I was getting carried away with myself. I started to laugh, forgetting I was in class. The teacher gives me that look, thinking I'm too immature to handle the topic of coital motion, so I straighten myself up. Pull it together. Sean must be thinking the same thing.

Anyway, so the bell rings and I get out of there fast. I take a few steps down the hall then stop. What are you doing? I ask myself. It's lucky blue jersey day. I turn around and see Sean. He's looking in my direction. No. He's looking dead at me. He's got that grin, watching me walk toward him. So, I can't believe I'm doing this. Going after the guy, when every guy goes after me, but it's now or not happening. So I kind of work my way through the hall crowd and say, "So Sean. You look pretty happy today."

God. The blue eyes are working. It's the whole blue on blue effect. The eyes, the Vince Carter jersey. He says, "I am," and he nods. Under the hallway light, the hair's got a little shine to it.

I'm trying not to drool. Still pulling myself together, I say something like, "Yeah, aren't you glad we're busting out of here early? You know, sixth period dismissal."

But I think I lost him. He goes blank, but he recovers. The Sean-ness comes back in full force. He says, "Wanna go out?" Like that. No rap. No nothing. Just cut right to it.

I'm like, wow. But I don't want to blow it. I haven't had a real moment since the seventh grade. This is real. I mean, I surprise myself. My grand plans are crumbling out from under me. I'm that nervous. Me. Raffina, "Miss-Quick-with-the-Quips." All I can manage is, "Sure."

I don't think he hears me. But he smiles and everything is all right. Then we walk out together. He says, "I mean, like on"—and then he hesitates.

Longest two seconds, ever. I'm already freaking, thinking, ON? ON WHAT?

"On a date type thing?" he says.

I contain the big sigh of relief. Slowly, Raffina comes back, confident and in control. "Yeah. I got that," I say. "But one thing. You gotta meet my brother Gary."

"You have a brother in this school?"

And there it is. Sean has no clue that I'm Gary's sister. I don't even think he knows who the Highlander Hero is. Just no clue. Don't you just love him?

SEAN + RAFFINA

by Terry Trueman

Her name is Raffina, pronounced "ruff-eena." I'm not even sure I'm spelling it right. Maybe it's spelled *Ruffina*, but I don't think so. I glanced at a homework assignment she turned in for Human Relations 2, and I'm pretty sure it was an *a* not a *u*. Whatever, it doesn't matter what her name is, or how she spells it anyway—what matters is that I wanna hit on her, and I'm not sure if I should or how to even start.

She'll be the first girl I've tried to ask on a date since I got TKO'd in the seventh grade. That's *if* I ask her. I'm not sure about that yet. If you'd been coldcocked by a petite blonde when you were thirteen, you might hesitate to think of yourself as God's great-red-hot-lover-boy gift to girls too. I owe my nondating history to Debra Quarantino.

Girls think I'm shy. I know that. I'm not all that shy, really—I just don't like making a fool of myself. Again, this is mostly thanks to Debra. It's amazing how quickly a thing can happen and change a person. One minute I was walking down the hall, full of myself and confident and feeling, in all my mostly pubescent glory, like a quasi-dude of a stud-muffin, and the next thing I knew, I was sitting on my ass wondering how a Mack truck had made it into Nicholas Murray Butler Junior High.

What had happened? All I'd done was run my finger down the middle of Debra's back. That was all. I remember she had on a white blouse and I could see her bra strap, and I'd seen other guys do the same little flirty trick with girls they'd liked. So I came up behind Debra and let my left index finger slide down the length of her little cute spine. Pretty funny, huh? Pretty James-Bond-hitting-on-Miss-Moneypenny cool, right? Not quite.

I never saw Debra's right hook coming. It caught me next to my left eye, which in a nanosecond was seeing stars. I honest-to-God had no idea why I was sitting on the hallway floor or how I'd gotten there.

I think I jumped up pretty quickly. I'm sure it was before a standing eight count would have been finished. Debra, maybe a little surprised by her own strength, just looked at me and said, "Knock it off!"

I said, "Okay."

It's not like everybody in school knew what had happened. I'm not sure anybody even saw. But when you're thirteen and this is how your first foray into the world of flirtation goes—well, most people would tend to be slightly careful afterward. "Slightly careful?" I could have joined a monastery for all the female action I've had these last three years.

The Debra knockdown punch is the excuse I've given myself for *not* asking anyone out until now, for not flirting with anyone until now.

Until Raffina.

So there's the Debra deal, but there's one other thing too.

I know this shouldn't be anything, shouldn't matter, but for some reason it does matter to me; Raffina is black, and I'm white. Of course, she's not really *black* any more than I'm really *white*. She's kind of dark brown, no, kind of medium brownish. I'm definitely sort of beige or something, light beige, tinted pink or red depending on how much time I spend in the sun (I don't tan; I just burn). Maybe a better way to put this is that Raffina's ancestors came from Africa, and my ancestors came from . . . I don't know . . . not Africa. Someplace like England or Germany or Canada or something.

Our school is mostly white kids. Make that beige kids. Has anyone anywhere ever been pure white? "Pure white," what the hell does that even mean? Like who? Queen Elizabeth of England? Eminem of Detroit? Debra Quarantino, flyweight champion of Butler Junior High? To even to say the words *pure white* together related to race is stupid, like I'm some kind of Nazi or Aryan nation idiot. But think about it: Debra was a white girl, somebody whose culture and stuff I knew, and look at how terribly things went with her.

Human Relations 2. That's the class Raffina and I are in together. Could there be any worse place in the universe to be sitting right next to someone you'd really like to hook up with than Human Relations 2? I mean, come on, we sit here every day from nine thirty a.m. until ten twenty-five a.m., and we hear about human reproduction. We sit about a foot apart, her arm next to my arm, her leg next to my leg, and in the front of the room is our teacher, Mr. Adams, talking. We're hearing all these words—*sperm, vagina, scrotum, penis, ovum*—I mean, damn. DAMN! How can you be cool and hit on a girl you like while you've got all that shit ringing in your ears?

If she wasn't African American, would I feel the same uncomfortable way about all these words being said in front of us together—*urethra, clitoris, labia, erection*? If it was Debra, how would I feel? Is it racist to even think about that or ask that question? I'm not being a smart-ass. I honestly don't know. People give other people shit for being politically correct. Nobody ever seems to think about how ignorant and full of crap you can sound if you *don't* pay any attention to what you say.

I know that race shouldn't matter. I mean, in terms of my thinking she's beautiful, in terms of my wanting to get with her, it sure doesn't make any difference, but the truth is that I just don't really *know* anything about African American people. Like I said, our school is almost all white. Shit, even our school team name is the Highlanders. Who the hell are Highlanders, like, Irish guys or something? The guy who jumps around with the cheerleaders at football games is a redheaded kid wearing one of those plaid skirts, and at really cold night games, his skin looks kind of light blue.

The thing is, I don't know squat about Raffina—not only on a personal, one-to-one basis, but on *any* level at all. What does she like to eat? Where does she live? What are her parents like, and how would they feel about their daughter hooking up with a white kid? Where would she like to go on a date if I ever got the balls to ask her? If Raffina was Debra, I'd just put on a video of *Rocky* and get the hell out the room. I know that I wouldn't ask

Raffina to watch *Gone With the Wind* or something like that where slavery was happening, but wouldn't it be kind of obvious and weird and like I was trying too hard if I slipped on a DVD of some "black" movie like *Barbershop* or *Boyz n the Hood*?

Now, say what you want, but if Raffina was white, I wouldn't be worrying about this kind of stuff. I'd still be worried about a Debra-like result, but not the race crap.

So why am I attracted to her? It's not because of the porno I've seen of black people having sex, 'cause I've seen porno of white people too, and both types of porno are equally sick and stupid and turn me on the same amount. I'm not attracted to Raffina because of her race, I'm attracted to her, well, just because I *am*. How can you explain attraction? She sits next to me in a class where we hear all this stuff about sex. I scoot my chair back from hers, just a few inches back, so that I can look over at her without her noticing. She has fairly large breasts and no gut and a nice butt and great legs. Okay, maybe that sounds shallow, but she does. I like to watch her chest as she breathes, the way her breasts rise and fall with each breath she takes. She's gorgeous, a thousand times sexier than Debra Quarantino, who after that moment in seventh grade always looked pretty tomboyish to me. I'm not gonna talk about the role Raffina plays in my late-night fantasies—I'll admit, though, that at those moments, color has nothing to do with anything. It's her parts—those breasts and legs and ass—and it's *her*, just how nice she is and funny—her laugh, her smile, her eyes. I like to think about us lying around after, like, after we've hooked up, just lying there talking and being together.

The main thing about Raffina is that she's always nice to me. Actually, she's always nice to everybody. Every day when we come into class, I always say hi, and she always smiles and says hi back. I ask her questions sometimes, even questions that I already know the answer to, just so I can be talking with her—and she always answers me. It's really hard to imagine her throwing a punch at me. Also, she's smart in addition to being good-looking and sexy. So, she's nice and smart and pretty—why the hell *wouldn't* I want to hook up with her? Why? Well, in addition to my memories of Debra, there's this one other little fact ...

Did I mention that my dad was born in Birmingham, Alabama, in 1948? Yeah, my dad's a bit on the older side. He was 46 when I was born and 48 when my sister came along. I was born in Alabama too, but we moved away when I was still a baby.

But in 1963, when Martin Luther King and the freedom marchers were trying to kick racism's ass, one of the worst atrocities against African Americans happened right there in Birmingham. Some white racists threw a bomb into a black Sunday school, killing a bunch of little kids. What if one of the guys who threw that bomb was related to my dad and me? What if my dad, who still lived in Birmingham back then, thought, for even a second or two that what happened at that church that day was all right? Could my dad be a racist too? I'm not just talking about white guilt here—my own or my dad's. Let me put it another way— my dad doesn't have a lot of Tupac posters or framed glossies of Dr. King up around the house (of course, he doesn't have any Slim Shady posters either).

I'm sitting at the dinner table with Dad and Mom and my little sister, who's two years younger than I am.

Mom's made a pot roast and potatoes, and we're having peas for a vegetable. Do black people eat this kind of food? What's a "collard green" anyway? I was born in Alabama, but I don't remember ever eating anything there.

We start to eat, and I decide this moment is as good as any.

"I'm gonna ask this girl out," I say, staring down at my plate the whole time.

"Oh, really," Mom says, a little too enthusiastically.

I flash on the thought, *Why the big surprise, did you think I was gay or something?* But I don't say anything.

Dad just keeps eating. He's got a forkful of peas balanced and ready to go into his mouth when I say, "She's black."

I glance at him quick to check his reaction. I'm wondering if any of the peas will fall off his fork or something. None of them do. He doesn't even hesitate to put the fork in his mouth.

Mom says, "Oh, that's nice."

I wonder, *What the hell does that mean?* I look over at her, and she's cutting a piece of roast with her knife and fork.

My little sister asks, "Why is she black?"

I say, "What?"

My sister says, "I mean, do you like her just because she's black, or do you like her for other reasons, too?"

I flash for a couple seconds on Raffina's breasts and smile and legs and how friendly she always is to me. I flash on us in bed together naked, just talking and being together after—

I say, "Other reasons, too."

My dad says, "That's good. She's a nice girl?"

"Yes."

"Good," Dad says.

My sister takes a mouthful of potatoes and, muttering, says, "I hope you have better luck this time than with ol' Debra Quarr-beano."

Why on earth I ever told my little sister about Debra's right hook, I'll never know—as I recall, when my sister got to seventh grade, she was being hassled so I told her. Let's just say there are some mistakes we never live down.

Mom, her ears all perked up, asks, "Debra who?"

I say, "Never mind."

But so much for Birmingham, Alabama.

So today's the day.

I want to get to Human Relations 2 a little early. I'm wearing a very cool North Carolina, light blue basketball jersey. I've never been to North Carolina. I've never even seen them play. But I like this shirt, the color and the way it fits me. I'm hurrying to get to class so that I can watch Raffina walk in, watch her body as she weaves her way through the desks and moves slowly toward me and sits down. I have this whole scenario planned out, where she'll look up and make eye contact with me and then I'll be sorta James Bond cool and hit her with the perfect line about going out.

Only when I get to class, she's already sitting there, and this turns my entire plan upside down. I smile through my nervousness, worried that I probably look like some moron with my gigantic, phony grin. She smiles back.

I drop my backpack onto the floor next to my seat and slide in. She looks really great, more beautiful than usual. But somehow all my brilliant lines, my grand plans disappear. I'm like some kind of mute.

We sit through the whole stupid class, and all I recall hearing are the phrases "coital motion" and "fetal nutrition." It amazes me that school can wreck anything . . . I mean *ANYTHING*! Finally the bell rings, and before I can even move, Raffina is out of her chair, heading for the door.

I feel so shitty, so cowardly, that I can't stand myself. For half a second, I wish I was a little kindergarten kid in that

Birmingham Sunday School and that I'd been blown up. Then I feel guilty and totally stupid for even thinking that way, so I gather my stuff up as quick as I can and hurry after Raffina. I see her in the hallway and manage to catch up, but just as I'm ready to reach out and touch her shoulder, I notice her beautiful dark skin under the white blouse she's wearing. I can see her bra strap too. I freeze like I'm in some kind of weird, drug-induced flashback. And suddenly, as if she's just sensed me standing there, Raffina turns around and walks toward me. I don't know what to say, so I force a smile again.

"You look pretty happy today," she says.

I feel the tiniest rush of confidence, and so I answer, "I am. It's a pretty great day." I think about finally getting up the nerve to ask her out, to hook up with her, to lie around in the afterglow, putting the ghosts of Debra Quarantino behind me forever . . .

Raffina laughs and says, "I know."

I hesitate. She knows? How does she know? What does she know? Does she know about Alabama? About Debra?!

I barely squeak out, "You know?"

"Sure, no sixth period today, early dismissal?"

I'd forgotten all about that. It's not important, but again, all my planned words just evaporate. I had my lines down perfectly, having practiced them over and over last night before I went to sleep. Now I'm all messed up again.

I mutter back a lame, "Oh, yeah, that too."

Now *she* looks confused for just a second, then asks, "What else?"

I try to find my place in my practiced speech; I try to figure how to start, where to start. I can't do it, can't remember anything.

She's staring at me, waiting.

I must look pathetic. I just say, "Nothing, really."

I think I see a flicker of disappointment in her expression. We're standing in the hallway with a thousand kids brushing past us, just like that day with Debra and the punch. But at this moment, I can only see Raffina. I *really* like her a lot.

It's now or never. "Wanna go out?" I ask, not too loudly, but not too softly either.

She's looking in my eyes, and I'm waiting. At least this time I'm braced and ready for a punch to land.

Softly, so low that no one else can hear her, she says simply, "Sure." And smiles again.

Suddenly everything I've been worried about seems ridiculous. She's a girl. I'm a guy. I like her and she—

I feel one last flash of doubt. "I mean like on . . . like on a date-type thing?"

She smiles again and gives a little laugh. "Yeah, I got that," she says.

In spite of myself, I can't stop from thinking, *Take that, Debra.* But in another few seconds, looking into Raffina's eyes as she looks back into mine, I realize that Debra Quarantino is the last person in the world I'll ever think about again.

MOUTHS
OF THE GANGES

by Terry Davis

Kerry is rhapsodizing about Mars. We park as many nights as we can get away, but we're here now, on this field access, danger-ously close to Kerry's midnight curfew, because it's the darkest place we could find with an open view of the southwestern sky where Mars hangs closer to Earth than it has in sixty thousand years. I told her this was a must-see. I lied. I wanted in her pants. I take delight in American English slang: *in her pants*. How do you not love the irreverence? I'd be all about *shoplifting the pooty*, like Jerry Maguire, if Kerry's pooty were shopliftable. Actually, the content of Kerry's pants is a long-range goal. It is *a consum-mation devoutly to be wished*, as Shakespeare says in *Hamlet*.

"Rafi," she says, "it's amazing. It's like a pearl on velvet, and the stars are spread out around it like tiny diamonds."

I'm burrowed into her breasts like a mongoose after a couple cobras of medium heft, so I know she won't hear me. I don't want to speak too loudly in case Homeland Security or INS has the Jeep bugged. You can only quote so much Shakespeare in the States. When the government hears about it, they cancel your visa.

... she hangs upon the cheek of night
Like a rich jewel in an Ethiope's ear.

Kerry scoots away. "What?" she says.

I look up at her, but I keep my head at breast level. All around the car, smells of farm country rise out of the land; it is the breath of Mother Earth. But in the front seat, in the few centimeters between my nose and Kerry's open blouse, the fragrance of baby powder remains after its release with the falling away of her bra. "These are the pearls I'm interested in," I say.

"Oh, you goof!" she says. "You're the one who got us out here so late, Mr. Let's Go Observe Mars." She hits me on the shoulder with her fist. I love it when she does that. Muslim girls never hit you.

I sit up. Two sentences later, we are into the sex confrontation we have four nights a week—the two nights our folks let us go out, and the two nights we're able to sneak. Kerry suffers more guilt in this than I do, although I have a lot more to lose if our families find out that we're this far over the line we swore to them we drew. I show her the tumescent crotch of my Carhartts.

"Poor baby," she says. She reaches. Her hand is a space probe entering the atmosphere of a planet where molten organic matter

124

courses in the substrata. The probe does not set down. I'm going to have to send out a probe of my own when I get home. Again.

My affection for Kerry is genuine. She is the furthest thing in the world to me from a *punchboard*, a *slut*, a *skank*, a *stain*, a *cooze*. I love this nasty American slang. And I love Kerry. I tell her I love her, at least, and in moments such as these, I believe with all my heart I do. I suppose a human being almost eighteen years old is capable of romantic love. We are certainly capable of erotic love, which seems to me a fair definition of this turgid heaven/hellish yearning. Of this *passion*.

I realize, technically, that the organ responsible for this passion is not my heart, but in spite of the anatomical distance between the organs, and their fundamental difference in shape, they often function as one.

Kerry made it clear months ago that she will go only so far. I tell my family that we hold hands; that's how big a liar and hypocrite I am. Premarital sex is a serious sin for Muslims. And I don't mean intercourse specifically; I mean any sex, period. My parents and my grandmother are devout, five-prayer-a-day Muslims. They're so strict they squeak. That is to say their knees literally squeak from all the genuflection. I myself am a quarter-prayer-a-week guy, and then it's only in fall and spring before races. And I go through the motions if I'm caught at home at prayer time. There may be no limit to my hypocrisy.

I respect the limit Kerry has set to our . . . to our love, and I'm grateful for it. God knows what trouble we'd be in if I was at the switch. The animal wants what the animal wants. Kerry's resolve bends, but it has not broken. Kerry is the one responsible for keeping our animals on a short leash. I do realize I'm responsible for my own animal, but I'm not sure it's healthy for him to be confined to so limited a range. I wonder why God created in us such powerful desires if he only wanted us to act on them under specified circumstances. It is a test of righteousness, and I fail.

"Let's head for home," I say. I slide Mix R, which Kerry hates, into the box. Tupac is up first: "Thug Passion," which Kerry double hates. She thinks I'm mad at her, but I'm not. I'm just . . . frustrated. I turn the key, hit the gas, and all four tires spin. My heart and that other organ sink in unison. We're stuck.

I drop Kerry off after getting pulled out of the mud in a surreal stroke of luck, and drive home in an aural bath of Da Lynch Mob's old-school outrage: "Freedom Got an A.K." Then Tupac is up again, and I rap along, idling down the two-lane blacktop through the deep buzz of this late-summer night, no po-leece chasin' me.

Of all the things my parents and my grandmother loathe about my love for America, they loathe the music with equal intensity.

I park a block down the street, sneak back like a slimmer, dark-haired, permanently tanned Chris Farley in *Beverly Hills Ninja*, hop the fence, and hit the latch on Muttski's kennel door. He stands with his paws on my shoulders and gives me a lick. I tell him we have a mission. We jump the fence and jog back to the Jeep.

I dial Mom on my cell and ask if *Dadi*—that's the Bangla word for Grandma; it's pronounced *Dah-dee*—needs anything from Hy Vee on my way home. It's my hope that Dadi cannot imagine me on a grocery run while simultaneously sustaining a vision of me ruining my future in the clutches of a *daughter of Satan*.

Dad and Dadi aren't pleased about me dating Kerry, but they haven't forbidden it, based on my stream of lies about our chaste behavior and my description of us as *friends*. They don't know her. Dadi doesn't need to know her; she's seen Kerry's photo in the school paper, she knows she's Christian and an American teenager, and that's all the info she needs to be certain that Kerry is not only a slut but a gold digger after my inheritance. Kerry hasn't got a clue how much money my family has, and wouldn't care if she knew. The diminutive endearment *dadi* sounds cute and sweet, but my little dadi is as hard as Abe Lincoln's noggin on Mount Rushmore.

Yes, Dadi is a bigot. My father is not, but he defers to his mother. This is odd, because outside the house Dad cuts a figure of authority and erudition. His accent is so deeply British it's almost Churchillian. He's a professor of agronomy at Iowa State: Dr. Vikram Mahdood. I think I've got them talked into meeting Kerry and her family tomorrow at the county fair. Once they meet her, I know they'll like her. I want to surprise Kerry, and I want to make an apologetic gesture for my behavior tonight. Dadi will be civil, but if she doesn't rise to graciousness, I'll introduce her to the pigs. *Dadi Mahdood, I would like to present Herbert, Gerbert, and Helga Hog.*

Kerry and I have been going out for two years now, and my mom's the only one who's met her. My family, and most of the other Muslims in Ames have kept a low profile since 9/11. The exception is another professor at ISU, Dr. Kamilla Jamini in women's studies. I'm also an exception, but it's not become I'm brave like Kamilla; I get attention because of cross country and track, and there hasn't been anything to do but go with it.

There are Muslim girls in Ames, where we live, but all the attractive ones go to the university. I never see them except once a year when Dad hauls us all to East Asia Night. He and Dadi stuck me in the little *consolidated* high school in Huxley, a tiny town ten miles south. They wanted to protect me from the drugs and violence in a big American school. Ballard High certainly isn't violent. But drugs . . . *they got a shitload a drugs there.* The first day of school, I met Kerry.

Kerry is America for me. She's that vibrant, athletic, hang loose, smart but not classically educated, funny, work hard and get dirty, oblivious to social class, ain't nothin' we can't fix personification of the American spirit. She carries a farming tool in her backpack. Kerry and America have really done a number on me.

And so has my dear Muttski Bear, who cruises with me to Hy Vee, where I pick up six big cans of chickpeas. That's garbanzo beans to the legume-challenged. I also sneak down aisle seven, where the baby powder nestles between the diapers and the wipes, just below the pacifiers, where I whiff the sweet redolence of Kerry.

Then we hit the car wash at Kwik Trip. I spray off all the mud and grass and vacuum inside while Muttski bites at the spray from the passenger seat. There are no lengths to which Dadi won't go to catch me beyond the parameters she and my father set for my behavior in America—academic behavior, substance-abuse behavior, and most particularly dating behavior that precludes the need for safe-sex behavior—so for her to conduct a DEA-style search of my car wouldn't surprise me. All she'll find now will be fresh Muttski fur.

I can't swing through Kwik Trip without looking at the spot between the front door and the caged racks of propane bottles, right below the water faucet, where I first set eyes on Muttski. It was the evening of September 14, three days after the attack on the World Trade Center. I was driving home from cross country practice and pulled into Kwik Trip for a Powerade. Every person in America who looked Middle Eastern was so self-conscious in those minutes and hours and days and weeks that our quaking probably registered on seismographs. The fact is that I don't look Middle Eastern. But you have to be familiar with different ethnic groups to recognize that, and most Americans—especially those who live in the heart of the heart of the country—aren't. People have spoken Spanish to me, thinking I'm Mexican. What I am, ethnically, is Bengali. People who have a sense of the world think I'm Indian—from India—which is the right ethnic group, but the wrong nationality. I've run into an amazing number of people who've never heard of Bangladesh.

I was having fearful thoughts about going back the first time I saw Muttski. My family didn't know what would happen to us. We didn't know if all Muslims would be deported or rounded up and detained in camps. We wondered if we should go back before the government had time to act. I didn't want to go home then, but I could have stood it; now going home would be the worst thing in the world for me. At the time I was scared. Beneath our fear, we were also confused. Muslims had been in the towers when they were hit, and Bangladeshis, too; plus, plenty of Muslims in America are Americans, either born or naturalized: We were so scared that our fear disrupted our compassion and our grief. It took people as mindful and tough as Kamilla Jamini to speak out in sympathy as anyone would to a neighbor whose loved ones had been murdered.

But when I saw the five fuzzy cinnamon-gold puppies peeking out from the Charmin box, my fear and self-consciousness fell away. I registered the boot steps behind me, but I paid them no mind. I looked at the boy and girl standing on each side of the box with the black crayoned FREE sign between them.

"They're free," the boy said.

"To good homes," the girl said.

An older biker, a big guy in a dark blue watch cap and a flannel shirt with cut off sleeves, sat on the cement next to the box. On his lap, a little boy in bib overalls squirmed in delight at the frenzied licks of the two puppies he held in his arms. The man leaned down. "These little muttski bears are smoochers, all right," he said. "We're gonna need a dozen shop rags to clean off all these guys' smooches."

I opened my mouth to exclaim about the puppies. They were beauty and joy and innocence made flesh and fur, in an ugly time when fear and sadness and mistrust hung over the world like a sickly green tornado sky. Before I could speak, I felt a hand clamp down on my shoulder. "What's up, Ahab?" said a voice I didn't recognize. I turned.

The man was in his thirties, shorter than I, but half again as broad. He wore dirty work clothes, and he smelled like Kerry's chicken house. The smell almost knocked me over. His face was so close I could have counted the individual red whiskers poking through the gray film of old powdered chicken manure. He wore a red, white, and blue NAPA auto parts cap exactly like the one I was wearing. He moved to speak again, but he stopped when he saw my cap. His mouth twisted into a snarl.

A sheriff's car wheeled off the street and bore down on us. I was watching it when the guy swung. He only knocked my cap off, but I fell back on the edge of the box. The biker bellowed, the three kids shrieked, and puppies yipped and catapulted into the air.

It sounds funny, but it's only funny from a distance.

The deputy extended his hand and helped me up. The kids gathered the puppies and straightened out the box; the biker soothed his little boy and their two puppies; the man in the NAPA hat and the grotesquely obese man who stood behind him like a chunk of landscape glowered at me.

"Ahab the Arab here was sneaking around the ammonia tank at the Co-op," the man in the cap said.

The deputy asked for my driver's license.

"The kid runs track at Ballard," the biker said. "I saw his picture in the paper."

"I'm on my way home from cross country practice," I said.

The deputy asked what I was doing at the Co-op. I had to think. The Co-op? Then it dawned on me. "I stopped to pee," I said. "I drove back where no one would see me."

"We saw ya," the huge man said.

"Yeah, and we called 911 and tailed ya here," said the man in the cap.

"Let's go back," I said. "There'll still be a wet spot in the dirt."

The deputy looked at the biker and his little boy, each of whom held a puppy. He looked down at the kids soothing their puppies in the box. He gave me back my driver's license, told the men who had followed me that it was time to head home to dinner, and he stood with us until they pulled away in their pickup. He told me that the next time I needed to *water my horse* not to do it near anything that could be stolen to make explosives. I thanked him. I meant for his kindness, but I was too nervous to get it out. He nodded and climbed in his car.

No one in my family—none of my older brothers or my sister, not my dad or mom, and none of the grandparents in my lifetime—has ever had a pet. Muslims don't have pets. So it was a big, big deal for me to take a puppy home. This, however, had been my desire when these little nuclear-fired balls of furry sunshine burst before my eyes. Now, though, I was afraid the kids wouldn't let me have one.

"If you give me a pup," I said, "I'll always be good to it, and I'll never leave it."

I picked the one with faint dark tiger stripes swirling through his cinnamon fur. I knew what I would name him.

The biker had put a pup in each of his saddlebags and buckled the straps. The pups had plenty of air, but they were crying mournfully. As I walked by, the little boy started to cry. He sat on the tip of the seat between his dad's legs. His dad leaned down. "I've got an idea," he said. He turned his head at me and smiled. "I bet this youngster here wouldn't mind giving our little mutt-skinzimmers a ride to our house in his car."

I held up my new little Muttski and said we'd be glad to.

Mom was the only one home when I walked in with Muttski peering out the neck of my coat under my chin like a baby-lion necklace. "Mother," I said, "I've done a . . . questionable thing."

My mother is a reticent, self-effacing Muslim wife, which is traditional. But she's that way as a mother, too, which is not. My older brothers and sister say she was a terror to them but that she wore out by the time I came along. I knew, however, that my little friend would get a rise out of her. It's hard for Muslims to imagine dogs as domestic, let alone bringing them in the house as pets. Back home the dogs are scavengers—they're feral and scary, and they can be dangerous.

She walked over to me from the kitchen doorway, her whole face in a squint. She wore an oven mitt on each hand and looked like she was training for a boxing match. "It looks so real," she said.

I lowered my eyes casually: Muttski was asleep. Before I could agree that, yes, the Americans were world-class stuffed animal makers, the door opened behind me and Dadi shot past me at typical Dadi speed with Dad moseying behind her. Mom helped Dadi off with her burka and folded it for her. There was nothing for me to do but step up.

"I have a dog," I said. "A puppy." Muttski woke up and squeaked as I held him through my coat.

Dadi and Dad looked at both of us as though we were sewer rats washed into our house in Dhaka City in the monsoon rains. I told them I would live on the patio with him until I could build a kennel.

I unzipped my jacket and held him up. "Look how clean he is," I said.

Dadi gave us an iron stare. "You are a boy who has no respect for his family or his culture," she said. I might as well have been holding a cobra. She walked through the kitchen to her room.

Dad stood his ground. "Rafi," he said, "that animal stays outside at all times. In our house you will obey the traditions and the rules of this family."

The Mutt and I drove back toward Huxley. I called Hank and Dave Thompson on my cell and used my Apu voice from *The Simpsons* when Hank picked up. "You are being congratulated lucky winner of one delicious chutney Kwik-E-Mart Squishee," I said. They go nuts when I do Apu.

"M'Dude!" Hank said. He drew it out: *M'Dooooooood*. He's the one who gave me the nickname. "'Sup, Bangladawg?" Dave said on the extension.

I asked if I could borrow a sleeping bag, and they said sure.

On the way home I bought puppy food in cans with pull tabs.

The baby Mutt and I were comfy tucked into the sleeping bag on the chaise lounge. I had my Walkman, my homework, my PowerBook, and sufficient light. Muttski had a can of water for a little drink and one of Dadi's yard shoes for a chew toy. I was happy, but I was starved. I kept thinking Mom would bring my dinner, but she never did. I Googled "Ahab the Arab" and found that it's an old novelty song by Ray Stevens. Ahab is sheik of the burning sand. At midnight he jumps on his camel named Clyde and rides across the desert to pillage. It's racist, I know, but it's hard to feel insulted by something that dumb. Kamilla Jamini, however, would be all over Ray Stevens like feculent odoriferousness on a nasty poo-poo stick.

Finally the lights in the house went out. I held a can of puppy food in my hand. My finger was in the tab when the back door opened quietly. Mom walked across the tiles with a steaming plate of lamb, rice, and eggplant. Had I been standing, I would have swooned.

Mom sat beside us while I ate. I was forced to give Muttski a second dinner so he'd leave me to mine. He lapped his water, then he curled into the shape—he was the approximate color—of a croissant, and fell asleep. Mom ran her finger lightly from the crown of his head to the tip of his shiny little wet black nose. I was touched by the tenderness in her face, and I remembered I'd seen this same tenderness before, back home when I was a little boy.

Bangladesh, in ratio of people to square kilometer, is the most populous nation on Earth. We also rank right up there in roadkill. Smooshed rats and mongooses and snakes and cats and dogs litter the roads. This is in dry weather, mind you. Monsoon season is a whole different kettle of fish. But when I was a little boy, there was no such thing as roadkill. I'd be on my mother's lap in the backseat of the car, my face pressed to the darkened window, my eyes peeled for the fresh horrors the highways offered.

"Oh, Mommie," I'd exclaim, "that one mongoose got smished as anything!"

And Mom would say, "Rafi, Rafi, Rafi. You thought that was a mongoose? I'm telephoning the ophthalmologist as soon as we arrive home. You are needing glasses, dear. That was a sweater in the road. You saw the red stripes and the brown?"

I had, in fact, seen red and brown.

And Mom would tell me that the driver of a sports car set out with that sweater tied around his neck, and he sped so fast that the wind lifted it from his shoulders and pulled at the arms till they unraveled from his neck. The sweater flew over the cars and trucks like a heavy woolen bird. "And so now," she'd say, "someone who can't afford a sweater will find this one, wash it up good, and have a lovely sweater to wear."

Mom conceived an article of clothing and the story of its loss for every dead animal I pointed out.

When Kerry points out a dead squirrel or a raccoon or a deer, I shake my head. I tell her it was a towel, a sweater, a really expensive winter coat exactly like one in the Land's End catalog.

I confided to Mom what happened at the Kwik Trip with the guys who followed me. I said I was glad the deputy showed up. She shook her head, and I saw that it scared her. I told her about the biker and his little boy, and giving their two puppies a ride to their house.

Mom touched her finger to Muttski's head again. This time she ran it along his spine to the base of his tail. Muttski twitched in his sleep.

"Rafi," she said, "do you know how dogs came into the world?"

I told her I didn't.

"Snuggle down and close your eyes," she said, "and I will tell you." She walked to turn off the patio light, then she sat back down.

I scooted Muttski up the bag and pulled him inside against my chest. I got comfy and closed my eyes.

"When God made Adam," Mom said, "the devil was furious because God looked upon Adam as his finest creation. God had made the devil of fire, and Adam of earth. The devil claimed that fire was a superior material, and that he was, therefore, superior to Adam. The harder the devil pressed his claim, the more his hatred for Adam grew. One day the devil and Adam were arguing, and he spit on Adam, right in the center of his belly. God was outraged to see the best of his handiwork defaced in this way. He reached down, pinched away the piece of flesh and threw it on the ground. An indentation remained in Adam's belly and in the bellies of all of Adam's offspring where God removed the flesh the devil had defiled. It looks like a little button."

I unsnuggled myself and looked up at Mom in the dark. "I thought you were telling me a dog story," I said.

She stood. "God looked at the little piece of flesh on the ground and did not want even one such small piece to go to waste. And so out of this profaned scrap of flesh God made the dog, whose duty it would be to clean up scraps forever."

I thanked Mom for the story and for bringing me dinner. I wished her good night as she pulled the door shut as quietly as a burglar.

I looked down at Muttski. I couldn't see if he was awake, but I hoped he wasn't because I didn't want him to have heard that demeaning story and to grow up with a crippled self-image. I pulled him close and whispered in his ear the true story of his origin. I spoke in Bangla, which I did a lot so he'd grow up to be bilingual, which he has.

Everybody thinks Adam was a guy full of confidence because he was God's favorite creation. But he wasn't as confident as everybody thinks. The truth is that Adam was lonely in the enormous new world all around him. Plus, the devil picked on him all the time. And plus again, the devil glowed ferocious with flames and brilliant shiny shimmers of heat, because he was made of fire, and Adam was made of the brown earth. The truth was that even though the devil was bad, he was beautiful, and Adam didn't feel beautiful. Plus, he was lonely in the enormous new world.

Once the devil saw that Adam felt inferior, his hatred for him grew. One day he was bullying Adam and his contempt boiled over. He spit on Adam—as all the stories tell—right in the center of his belly.

But here's where all the stories get it wrong.

The devil's spit was volcanic, and it burned that hole in Adam's belly. Why didn't God blow on it to cool it off? Because God wasn't around right then, that's why. And the devil knew it. That's something else the other stories get wrong: God isn't always around.

When God came back, he found Adam sitting on a smooth round rock staring into the fiery sunset. Adam was feeling that everything in the world was brighter and stronger than he was. This wasn't true, but that's how Adam felt, so that was the world he saw. God looked into Adam's heart and saw all of this.

God walked with Adam far from the devil's radiance and roar. God reached into Adam's heart and excised a little piece. He pointed to a patch of earth where flecks of pure gold lay on the surface like tiny leaves. "My son," God said, "I'm going to make a new creature who will always love you." God scraped up a palm full of the golden earth and mixed it with the piece of Adam's heart. He wrung his hands together and molded the heart-earth into a ball the color of cinnamon. He rolled the ball out on the ground. It sprouted four legs, a tail, pointed ears, a bright, curious face radiant with love, and a noble snoot. The dog ran up to Adam and licked his foot where Adam had stepped in something nasty. It tickled, and in a few licks Adam's foot was clean. Adam smiled. The dog smiled. God smiled. And Adam had a friend forever.

I told that story to my new little Mutt, and he's always acted like he took it to heart.

There's a problem with the story, though, and I thought about it as I lay there. What about the scar that should have marked the center of Adam's chest where God reached into his heart? We know that scars are lessons. How come Adam didn't have that scar on his chest for us to inherit? I think it's because the wound created by feeling like a dark thing in the world is the deepest wound of all. And the lesson is that the scars of the deepest wounds don't show. We carry them inside.

Dad got me up the next morning before my run. He was already dressed in his suit and tie. No tea, no breakfast, no brushing teeth. I thought he was mad at me because of Muttski, who had already done two enormous poo-poos on the lawn. But he seemed more preoccupied than mad. We climbed in the car, then we were walking into the police station before I'd dug the sleep out of my eyes. Dad had a death grip on his briefcase. He asked to see the person in charge, and we were taken to the watch commander. The man asked us to sit, but Dad was too agitated. He introduced himself and opened his briefcase. He gave the man our passports, then he introduced me and made me hand over my Ballard ID. He pulled a newspaper clipping from his wallet; it was the photo of me from the sports section of the Ames paper. Everything since he walked outside and woke me up had been weird, but him saving any reference to me as an athlete was the weirdest thing of all. I listened to him say that I ran every day, all over town, and often after dark—and that was when I got it: Mom had told him about the guys calling 911 on me. Dad was scared that the police would see me running and think I was running away from something. Out of his case he pulled a Kinko's sack, and out of the sack a sheaf of photocopies of the newspaper photo. He wanted every cop in Ames to know I was a high school runner, not a member of an Al-Qaeda sleeper cell. The man took the copies, shook our hands, told us not to worry, and wished me good luck in the rest of our meets.

On the way home, Dad told me that if Dadi'd had her way, he'd have been driving me to Des Moines to put me on a plane for home. I told him I was glad I wasn't going home. He said he never wanted me out on a night run without a reflective vest and to take "that dog" with me.

And then my father surprised me as he had never before. We were passing a Kwik Trip, and he looked over. "Ah," he said, "I see the Kwik-E-Mart. Perhaps I am treating my son one Squishee."

I thought the smile would stretch my face out of shape forever. "Oh, yes," I replied, "one delicious carp Squishee would be hitting the spot."

We talked Apu English from *The Simpsons* the rest of the way home. I'd never heard him speak anything but Oxford English before or since.

I'm smiling with this memory of my father bending linguistic decorum as I bounce through the back door with my quadrupled plastic Hy Vee bag of garbanzos a few minutes after final prayers. I remind everyone that tomorrow is the Story County Fair and that they've said they would meet Kerry and her folks. Actually, what they've said is "we'll see."

I sit down with Dad at the kitchen table and take a little swig of his tea. Mom pours her tea at the counter. Dadi walks by and pinches my pierced ear. It's been a year, and she still can't set eyes on that tiny, harmless aperture without her venom rising. She'd have a stroke if she ever saw my hoop in. She'd never have noticed it that first time, but it was still a little red, and I made the mistake of telling her it was a zit. She came after my head squinching her eyes and pinching her thumbs together like an amateur dermatologist at a middle school chocolate buffet. It was horrible. "You've got it, Dadi," I said. "I'm sure you've got it all now."

There was hardly anything left of my ear lobe when she realized that "the core" was not just deep; it went all the way through. I was afraid she and Dad were going to deport me for sure that time.

Dad and I wish Dadi sweet dreams, and I rub my ear. Mom sits down.

I tell Dad that Kerry heard Smithville Pork was building a huge new hog operation just down the road from Hank and Dave Thompson's farm. I hate lying, and yet I lie all the time. I say I thought the zoning commission voted to keep hog factories out of Story County. Dad goes to all those meetings, and he knows Gordon Smith.

"No," Dad says, "the commission tabled that resolution pending an environmental study."

"Nothing to study in that location," I say. "A zillion gallons of hog waste into Ballard Creek and on into the Skunk River. Game over for the aquifer."

"Where did Kerry hear this?" Dad asks.

I tell him, "I don't know. She probably heard it from Hank and Dave, who are conspiracy psychos when it comes to agribusiness. I'm headed out to sleep with Muttski. Good night."

Muttski is so big now that we can't fit together on the chaise. I made a plywood platform that I toss his dog bed on, and I scoot it up so we're side-by-side. I bought two sleeping bags; I sleep in one, and I open the other and throw it over both of us. We're snug as bugs in a rug.

I confess that the touch of his long soft hair on the skin of my arm makes me think of Kerry. It's not only that Muttski's hair is the same color as Kerry's; it's the same ethereal texture. He doesn't smell nearly as good, though.

I fall asleep happy—I think I'm happy, that is, but I must not be, because I dream of the Mouths of the Ganges. It's monsoon season. The rains have been torrential, and the flooding is catastrophic. My two uncles, who are in charge of flood relief, have taken me out in their government boat. They believe I should see the devastation. The boat is big and safe. My father is glad for me to go so I can observe another aspect of government service. In time, he contends, when I return from university, I will serve our country. I am ten years old. The dream is just as it was when I lived it.

We are many kilometers south of Dhaka in the tidal forest swamp that covers the entire southern coast of Bangladesh even in the dry season. We started the day on the river, but as we came south, the river and the flood waters merged into an ocean of debris. Take a filthy flooded street, add more garbage and bodies of all living creatures from babies to the aged, then make it the size of a country. I saw a five-meter crocodile stuck in a culvert pipe; I saw a cobra swim over the back of a cow. I couldn't tell a dead baby from a rubber doll. Survivors clung to trees, telephone poles, and the roofs of submerged cars, and huddled in the scattered houses built on pilings. The back of the boat was full of these people, a number of whom died there of snakebite. All afternoon I helped a young seaman knock the snakes off the boat's gunnel with an aluminum pole. When night fell, my fear got the best of me and I climbed up and sat on a stool next to the helmsman.

I dream this nightmare often. I've dreamed it—off and on—for almost eight years. It's a mix of memory and dream, and the dream part is always set in the deep of night. Our boat's searchlights sweep the darkness, and their beams intersect with the lights of other boats. I know the bodies and the snakes and the crocodiles are out there, but only the seamen along the gunnels see anything.

Tonight, though—for the first time—I'm at the gunnel, and what I see in the black water below are Kerry and Muttski, floating . . . like beautiful drowned things. I try, but I cannot make them lost articles of clothing.

I had heard the term *Mouths of the Ganges*, and I had been there and—supposedly—seen them for myself. But all I'd really seen was water. So when my uncles took me back home, I looked in the *World Book* at a map. And then I saw why the region is called by that name: From southwestern India all along our coast with the Bay of Bengal are inlets that look like mouths. Some are narrow and come inland just a short way; others are wider and cut deeper into the land. But every one of them looks like a mouth, and from that day forward, I have been afraid that eventually these Mouths of the Ganges would devour me.

I've been spooked all day. The dream has never scared me this bad. I gave Muttski extra portions of love while I fixed a cargo net to the back of the Jeep so he could ride there without reaching Mom and Dadi in the rear seats to give them kisses with his big purple tongue. It turns out that giant Muttsker Bear is part Chow. And something really big and with the possibility of being light colored, maybe Great Pyrenees.

I've e-mailed Kerry that we are coming. I included a poem I'd sent her before, in my first note to her. I felt like saying it again, and I wanted something from my own culture. I signed it as I'd signed it before. She told me one night after a cross country meet that I ran like silk.

> *Like a silkworm weaving*
> *his house with love from his marrow,*
> *and dying in his body's threads*
> *winding tight, round and round,*
> *I burn desiring what the heart desires.*
> —*The Silky Worm Guy*

I know what moved me to dream: It was the lights of the earthmovers Kerry and I saw. They must have clicked with my memory of the searchlights on the boats. What I'm going to be devoured by is this freaking dream.

I drive slowly through the light afternoon traffic. We must look a sight to our Iowa neighbors: two women covered in black burkas; a Bengali man with a little Apu mustache riding shotgun; me at the wheel in my Iowa State cap; and Muttski in back wearing his Cyclones kerchief, looking like a fat cinnamon bear pleased to have been abducted from the circus in a bright yellow Jeep, top down.

It's a big deal for Mom and Dadi to come to the fair. I chose the fair because it's the most conservative get-together I can think of with families—besides church. There's no midway, just the 4-H projects, so it'll just be farm kids. Few bare bellies, not many piercings or T-shirts that will shock women who live in a tradition of immense public modesty. And not many public displays of affection, I hope.

I think of Mom, who after two years finally comes to my meets. Mom doesn't drive, so she has to call someone for a ride. Sometimes Kamilla brings her, but sometimes she calls one of the other mothers. It wouldn't be a big deal for a lot of women, but it's a big deal for my mom. She stands along the course, or in the bleachers, surrounded by chants of "Dood, Dood, Dood, M'Dooooood!" as her son runs by wearing an earring and a hemp necklace.

I hate lying to a woman who does this for me. After two years I'm still telling them that Kerry and I go to the library to study. Can they possibly believe me?

And the things unsaid—which are lies, too—are building up. It is understood that I'll attend university in England next year and study agronomy, as Dad did, or business like my uncles. But the truth is that I want to study literature in the States, and I want to run. And running means a smaller, less prestigious school, Division II or maybe Division III.

I'm sick to death of lying. It's the lies that are going to devour me.

MARS
AT NIGHT

by Rebecca Fjelland Davis

Mars looked like I could pluck it from the black ceiling over our heads.

"Look, Rafi," I said.

"I'm looking," he mumbled into my chest.

"I meant at the stars, you goof. At Mars." I was hoping to distract him from burrowing further under my clothes, from his hands on my breasts, but it wasn't working. I didn't really want him to stop. I loved every inch of him, and I wanted to get lost in this sea of touch and ride the waves on and on. Everything else, Mars included, fell away.

I pulled his head against my chest. My bra, unhooked, was up around my neck with my tank top, and I stroked the curly dark hair he kept cropped close to his skull. I felt myself shiver in spite of the sultry night when he moved his fingers, tracing where my bra had been fifteen minutes ago. My body arched against him, even though some place in my brain was screaming for me to be careful.

So I turned my brain off at these moments. If I didn't, I could hear my grandma's voice, like ice water dumped from one of her heirloom crystal goblets, spilling all over my half-naked body. Sometimes I forced myself to remember Grandma, hoping the ice water would stop me cold, give me the strength to say no.

"You give a boy what he wants, it's fornication. I don't care if he is the student body president and track star, tennis star, if his daddy is the most respected dean at Iowa State. And if you marry that boy, you marry his family. That's when you'll know he's a Muslim, even if you say it doesn't matter. He might want you now, but those Muslims don't respect their wives. You mark my words, and you don't get too involved with that boy. I don't care how handsome he is. There's no end but a bad one if you fall in love with that boy."

"We're just friends, Grandma," I had protested.

"Friends, my foot," Grandma said. "I see how you look at each other. It's downright sinful."

I memorized the lecture because Grandma spouted variations of it every time Rafi's name came up, every time he came over when Grandma was around.

"Your grandma doesn't like me much," Rafi had said.

I felt myself shudder again. Sometimes, when Rafi touched me, his toffee-colored fingers on my skin, only my guilt was bigger than my desire to pull all of Rafi's beautiful body inside my own. Then guilt and Grandma jolted me back to reality and I panicked. Terror of going too far and getting caught. I sat up. I tried to pull Rafi's head up to kiss him, to distract him from my boobs and everything below.

He was a magnetic force, and pulling away physically didn't work. I leaned my head back to try talking. "Look at Mars, Rafi. It's amazing. It's like a pearl on velvet, and the stars are spread out around it like tiny diamonds."

Rafi mumbled something else into my chest.

"What?" I said, trying to scoot out of reach.

He looked up at me. "These are the pearls I'm interested in."

"Oh, you goof!" I said. "You're the one who got us out here so late, Mr. 'Let's Go Observe Mars.'" I smacked him on the shoulder, but not hard.

He sat up.

"Rafi, look at Mars."

"Oohh," he groaned, flopping back against the driver's seat. He reached down to rearrange the overstrained crotch of his jeans. "Mars is the god of war, you know."

"Great," I said. "Just great. War looks like a pearl when it's far enough away."

I tried to lean against him, but he pulled sideways, away from me.

I bit my lip. "I'm sorry," I said.

He made a fist on his own knee, then made himself relax. "You make me crazy." He reached toward me and ran a shaking hand down my thigh below the hem of my skirt, the other hand still on his crotch. "You just drive me nuts, you're so beautiful. You make me ache."

"I just feel so guilty. Rafi, I can't—"

"I know, I know." He huffed, leaning back and looking at the stars, too. "They're so bright, it makes me understand why van Gogh painted them the way he did."

"Hmmmm." I nuzzled back onto his shoulder. "That's a romantic thing to say."

"Must have been a woman driving him crazy," Rafi said. "I never thought of that before. That's probably why he went insane."

He sat up so suddenly that my head slipped off his shoulder, a whiplash withdrawal. "Well, let's get going. I can't stand to sit here with you and not touch you."

He stepped on the clutch and turned the Jeep's ignition key. I flopped my head back on the seat, hating the stars, the war god for being desirable from a distance.

The Jeep engine ground to life and our night ground to a stop. As if the stars had come crashing down. I leaned forward and hooked my bra, tugged at my skirt. Next Rafi wouldn't be able to get me home soon enough. He'd shut down and left me with an emptiness as big as a sky devoid of stars.

There was no end to this guilt. Guilt for going so far. Guilt for not going all the way, for driving Rafi nuts. Guilt for not being able to tell Grandma and Mom and Dad the truth. A sea of guilt where I had to tread water to breathe.

Tonight still hung muggy after last night's thunder, lightning, and torrential rain. The Skunk River and Ballard Creek had flash-flooded, there'd been so much rain—four inches in four hours. But the air hadn't lost any of its heaviness, in spite of the storm.

Mosquitoes were torrential, too. I swatted, glad to have something to smack, and glad we would be moving soon.

I pushed the damp hair from my forehead and leaned farther back, aching, wondering how it would feel to be driving home if we'd had sex after all. I couldn't feel much worse.

Rafi didn't seem eager to have my head on his shoulder. I was glad that he had a Jeep convertible so at least I could watch the stars—the stars that hadn't come crashing down after all, but made a sort of net to suspend me here. I waited for him to buckle his seat belt, to ride home through the summer night air and cool our bodies from our own heat and the heat of this beastly July day. Not speaking.

He put the car into first and stepped on the accelerator. The Jeep spun and lurched forward less than an inch, spinning on the slick dirt road, muddy from yesterday's downpour. I lurched in the seat.

"What the . . . ," Rafi muttered.

He slipped it into reverse. Same thing. First gear again. More spinning. I could feel the Jeep grinding itself further into the muddy ground. I sat, silent, staring straight ahead. I wished he hadn't already been mad at me when this happened. I wanted to touch him, but I felt like he'd slammed that door shut. He tried rocking back and forth six more times before he put the car in neutral.

"Oh, oh." He touched his forehead to the steering wheel. "Just the perfect way to end the night." He muttered something else I couldn't hear. I didn't ask him to repeat it.

I bit my lip. "I didn't realize it was that muddy when we drove in here."

"Man," Rafi exploded, and turned the ignition off. "I was not even *thinking* about the terrain while I was trying to drive in here and keep my hands on you. Shoot. You're the farm girl. You should have thought of this."

"Rafi! This is *not* my fault. *I* was a little distracted, too."

"I know, I know. Sorry. Okay, I'll go get somebody to pull us out of this mess."

"Thompsons," we said in unison.

"You want to sit here and be mosquito bait, or do you want to walk to Thompsons' with me?" He was getting out while he asked, not making eye contact with me.

To answer, I jumped out of the car. I was wearing only a tank top, skirt, and sandals, so walking out of here on the deserted muddy road, then down the gravel road wouldn't be much fun. But I wasn't about to just sit here alone until the mosquito hordes dive-bombed me into a mass of welts.

Harvey Thompson and his wife and sons, David and Hank, lived half a mile away, the only near neighbors on the gravel road. They had a huge dairy farm and raised one of the largest crops of pigs around. They farmed the whole section on the opposite side of the gravel road and used the pasture bordering Ballard Creek to keep the cattle satisfied.

Hank and David were both in high school with us and in my 4-H club. I felt my face blush in the dark, anticipating them coming to the door, grinning at us while they hooked chains from their John Deere 3020 to the Jeep to pull us out.

And even if the Thompson boys didn't meet us at the door, they would know the story by tomorrow morning. Tomorrow happened to be the day the whole county was scheduled to bring 4-H livestock projects to the county fair. Even if I could escape them tonight, I *would* have to face both David and Hank Thompson tomorrow. Knowing them, they'd settle their show heifers into the dairy building and make tracks over to the hog barn, where I would have my pigs, just to smirk at me and taunt. All in all, they would be good-natured about it, as long as I didn't die of embarrassment. And better them teasing me than my own parents finding out, and, heaven forbid, my grandmother.

This was a primo secluded parking spot, since there were twenty uncultivated acres here, bordering a runoff ditch and stream that usually trickled but now roared through a culvert under the gravel road, joined Ballard Creek on the Thompsons' property, and flowed in it, now brimming its banks, all the way to the Skunk River five miles away. Here the grass was wild, since it went uncultivated and ungrazed, and after spring rains, the ground was so spongy nobody had tried to grow anything here for as long as I remembered.

It was the first time I had ever gotten stuck parking.

Rafi was striding, fast, on his long, lean eight-hundred-meter-champion legs, but I managed to keep up.

"Look," I said finally, grabbing his hand, "I know you're mad at me. I'm sorry, but I feel so blasted guilty that it's just gonna take me a while, okay? I hear my grandmother in my head when . . . you know. I'm sorry."

We kept walking. Rafi didn't say anything, but at least he didn't pull his hand away.

"I want it too, you know," I said. "I just can't quite go . . . all . . . the way."

We walked a little more, and I could feel the rigidity slip away from his hand. "I'm sorry I was a dick," he said finally.

I squeezed his hand.

"I feel guilty too, you know. It's just . . . " He finally looked at me, for the first time since we put the brakes on our steamy skin, and said, "you turn me on so much. You drive me nuts, and I guess I can't stop—"

"Well, try, okay? I hate it when you're like this. It's not fair."

"I'm sorry." He squeezed back. We reached the gravel road and turned toward Thompsons'. The yard light was on, but no house lights that I could see. It was, Rafi checked, eleven forty.

"Oh, yum," said Rafi. "Smell."

I breathed in through my nose. Hog and dairy cattle smells. "Smells like home. Some people would say it smells like money."

"Yuck. I couldn't get used to *that* smelling like home. Makes me glad I don't eat pork."

We had only walked about fifty yards on the gravel road when an army of bright headlights turned from the highway onto this gravel road, over a mile away. It's so flat in this part of Iowa, we could see three or four miles most any given time, any given direction. We kept watching as one, two, three, four, five, six big machines of some unidentifiable shape in the darkness turned from the highway onto the gravel road and lumbered straight toward us, lights flooding the road and ditches. The unmistakable diesel engines throbbed louder by the second.

"What the heck?" My throat felt like it was closing up. Whatever was coming at us filled the road, and it seemed we'd have to take the ditch just to avoid being plowed over. By the time the front headlights flooded us, my feet stopped. I pulled Rafi with me over to the side of the road, almost into the ditch. This was like a creepy science fiction movie. It was unheard of in the middle of the summer, in the middle of the cornfields, in the middle of the night, to bring six giant machines to the fields. For one thing, corn was too tall to drive through, but after plowing, planting, cultivating, and spraying, farmers could take a breather while they watched their crops grow ready for harvest. July and August were when farmers could take a few days off—the only time they could take summer vacations—and that's why county fairs and state fairs, too, had been scheduled in late summer since time began.

We stood there frozen as the headlights bore down on us. The light beams lit us up like we were on stage. In spite of the damp roads, the machines kicked up enough gravel dust to make us cough. We covered our mouths against the dust and squinted against the blinding light of this monstrous midnight parade.

The headlights slowed as they pulled even with us, and we turned like weather vanes, to see the first machine as it passed. Then we could finally make out a huge orange Caterpillar earth-moving machine. At midnight? I shaded my eyes from the second set of headlights to try to see the first driver. The parade slowed to a crawl, and the first behemoth ground to a stop. Right beside us.

"You kids okay?" The voice was friendly enough, not demonic as I had started to fear, feeling like Rafi and I had gone parking inside a Stephen King novel. When I could make out the guy's face, I could see a dirty Twins baseball cap over leathery skin and brown eyes that twinkled. "You okay?"

"Freaked out," I finally said. "What are you *doing*?"

"Just getting equipment ready for morning. Boss wanted it here before six a.m., so we decided to move it now instead of getting up at four."

"What for?" Rafi asked. He slipped his arm around my shoulder. It made me feel a tiny bit safer, but only a tiny bit.

"Building a foundation."

"For what?" I asked.

The guy shrugged. "We just do what we're told," the guy said, looking in a rearview mirror to check his convoy. "So, why you kids walking?"

"We're stuck," Rafi said. "Just at the end of that dirt road. See?" He pointed.

The guy squinted in the direction of the Jeep, smirked, and nodded. Its chrome roll bars reflected the machine's headlights. "Ah. Well, you're in luck, kid. That's where we're headed. That's the dirt road where we start clearing for a foundation in the morning. So I reckon this little thing can pull your car out of the muck."

"Wow. Thanks." Rafi grinned.

I let out my breath in relief. We wouldn't have to wake up the Thompsons after all. Mrs. Thompson wouldn't tell half the county that Rafi and I had gotten stuck parking.

"Want to ride?" the guy asked.

Rafi eyed the ladder and then looked at my short skirt. "Maybe we'd better walk."

"Joe, third one back there, has a cab. Maybe you can get in with him." The guy picked up some sort of walkie-talkie and held the button. Through some static, he said, "Joe? Can you give these two kids a lift? Their car is stuck right where we're headed."

So Rafi and I waited, holding hands, and then we scrambled up into the cab of the earthmover third in line.

"Name's Joe," the guy said. Rafi and I nodded. That was the only thing we already knew. He looked considerably less dirty than the first guy, even if his eyes weren't quite as bright.

"Nice to meet you. Thanks for the ride," Rafi said. I was grateful he didn't volunteer our names.

"Nice night," the Joe guy said. "Stars and all. Good night for a deserted road." He winked at Rafi. I saw it and felt myself get hot in the face.

It also pissed me off, that guys could have this instant cama- raderie if sex was involved, so I said, "What are you guys doing? I mean, what are you building? Way out here, deserted road and all. Why are you sneaking in here at midnight?"

"Hog barn. Big operation. Something like twenty thousand hogs. I'm not really sure of any more than that."

"Hogs?" I felt my jaw slagging open. "*Twenty thousand hogs? Who's building it?*"

"Smithville Pork," the guy said. "We just go in and clear the place and get it ready and lay the foundation, and then somebody else comes in to do the rest."

"Hogs?" I felt pinched in the middle, sick, as if somebody had put a vise grip on my stomach. I had heard about big hog facto- ries that came bulldozing into a nice quiet farming community, putting local little pig farmers right out of business and pouring thousands of gallons of waste into the rivers, instead of using manure spreaders to put it back on the fields like family farm- ers always did. Here was a hog factory two miles from my house. Two miles from my own pigs and from my dad's hog barn, where we had maybe 180 baby pigs in a season. Twenty thousand hogs. I looked at Rafi. He was reading my face, and we were quiet.

The whole army plowed up the dirt road and parked. The first one nosed up to the Jeep. Another worker extracted a long chain from a toolbox on his Caterpillar, hooked it under the Jeep and to the Cat. "Jump in," he said, so Rafi jumped, turned on the motor, and the Jeep sprayed some mud and popped free in less than three seconds.

"Thanks. Thanks a lot," Rafi said while I stood there in the weeds, swatting mosquitoes.

"You kids be good now," the lead driver said. He winked at Rafi in the headlights.

I jumped in and we drove down the dirt road toward the gravel. I watched behind me as one by one, the monsters shut down their lights and their motors. The next-to-last vehicle in the caravan was a cement truck, and the last was a big SUV. All the drivers piled into it. After the roar of the caravan, the motors of only the Jeep and the SUV in the darkness seemed like silence.

I stepped into the house, trying to be noiseless. I'd missed my midnight curfew by ten minutes, but that was pretty good considering all that had happened. Nobody woke up, or at least nobody got up to yell at me, so I stripped off my clothes, pulled on a T-shirt and boxers, and fell into bed.

I couldn't fall asleep. I lay there, feeling Rafi's hands on me, his mouth, his fingers, and aching, and getting interrupted by blinding diesel headlights. A hog factory. A hog factory. When I finally slept, I dreamed of a giant hog on wheels with its huge mouth wide open, creeping closer and closer to our hog barn. I came awake and when I slept again, the giant pig was creeping up on my 4-H pigs, ravenous mouth open to consume them.

Dad woke me at five thirty, and I guess I sat up crying, "Get away!" The sound of my own voice brought me to my senses. Dad teased me about yelling in my sleep.

"I was dreaming . . ." I started to tell him about the dream, but when I got fully conscious, I realized that if I told him about the hog factory, he would know Rafi and I were parking. There would be *no* other reason for us to be on the Thompsons' road. So I shut my mouth and just looked at his face. He had already shaved, and he was still grinning at me. I took my pillow and swung it at him.

"Dad?" He needed to know about the hog factory. Today. Before they got the foundation laid. But there was no way to tell him without talking about where Rafi and I had been.

"Yeah?" He stopped, waited.

I looked at him, and I couldn't do it. "Nothing. I'm nervous."

He nodded and disappeared down the steps.

Yesterday, we had washed my three market hogs, two barrows (male pigs who were castrated to be raised for meat, not breeding) and a gilt (a young sow, called a gilt until her first litter), and had bedded them down in an overabundance of clean straw so they would be clean for this morning. Dad already had the pickup and trailer backed to the hog house. My little brother Dean's single barrow was ready, too. This was Dean's first year in 4-H, and he was so excited he was bobbing up and down at the breakfast table. At five thirty-five in the morning, going on too little sleep and the near nausea that came with it, I wanted to bop him in the head. Much to my credit, I didn't.

Mom was silent while we ate. Dean skipped out of the house after gulping his eggs and orange juice.

"Kerry." Mom stopped me while I was trying to dodge out the door after Dean. "What time did you get home last night?"

I took a deep breath. "Twelve ten," I said. "Sorry." Lying was pointless. Mom set such traps. If you tried to lie yourself into good favor by pretending you hadn't broken a rule, you'd get double-whammied because she already knew the answer before she asked the question. Mom looked me in the eye, guilt barbs in full force. "I'm disappointed in you."

"Sorry, Mom."

"No late nights at the fair for you."

I wanted to tell her about the hog factory. Mom and Dad *needed* to know. Plus, it would get me out of hot water for being late, but it would get me into the fire for parking, so being late was the better of the two evils. I'd stay in the hot water. I kept my mouth shut.

"Kerry. You *have* to be careful with that boy. I didn't want to forbid you to see him, but I'm afraid I'll have to."

"*Mom.* We're not . . ." *doing anything*, I wanted to say but couldn't. I didn't know if that was true. We were, after all, *doing something*, just not as much as we could be or wanted to. Not as much as some of my friends were doing with their boyfriends. Sally, for instance, who had just started birth control pills.

I didn't have to finish my sentence. Mom turned her back on me, silent, busying herself with dishes. The famous silent treatment.

"I'd better go, Mom." I kissed her cheek. Mom nodded but didn't kiss back, didn't lift her face.

We loaded the pigs into the stock trailer. Doing familiar labor with Dad and Dean was a comfort, and I was glad I wouldn't have to face Mom again until evening.

As we drove, the smell of summer filled the pickup cab. "Smell that corn growing," Dad said. "Do you know anything as sweet?" I took a deep whiff. It was a rich, earthy, green and moist smell that indeed did smell like growing.

"Hay smells even better," Dean volunteered.

Dad grinned at him. "Well, for today, the corn is the best smell in the world. On baling day, hay is the best smell."

"Dad," I started, "is there a hog factory going in around here?"

"*That* would stink things up. Wouldn't be able to smell summer anymore. No, there's not. Why?"

"I—heard there was."

"Nope. Farm Bureau meeting in March, remember? Gordon Smith promised us that the lobbyists had been so powerful that the Zoning Commission ruled to keep hog factories out of Story County. Remember?"

I nodded, and the knot in my stomach twisted back in place. Dad deserved to know. "Dad, there's . . . " Dad was smart, and if I said anything, he would know instantly that I had been parking at the end of the dirt road with Rafi's hand under my bra. And if he knew, then Mom would know, and Mom made her rules based on Grandma's rules. And I might not get to see Rafi at all.

"Yeah, Ker?"

"Nothing. Just that this is the best smell in the world."

I could mesmerize myself, watching the fields. Watching perfectly even, straight rows of corn zip past my eyes was the same sensation as running a thumbnail over the teeth of a comb.

We drove to Nevada to the fairgrounds, signed in our hog projects at the registration building, received our official white and green fair T-shirts to wear while showing our animals, found our pen assignments, and unloaded the four pigs into two pens with fresh wood chip bedding. We put the bags of Supersweet hog feed inside their white wooden box stenciled with green four-leaf clovers and our names. I padlocked the box. Dean filled a bucket at the hydrant outside the barn and poured water into a trough in each pen, and then he took off to find his buddies.

I sat on the fence under our 4-H club name sign—PALESTINE PEPPY PUSHERS—trying to get the pigs to calm down a little. They were so wound up, it was as if a giant hungry pig really was after them. Dad put his hand on the small of my back. "They're lookin' good, Ker. You've done really well. Could be, should be, your year to take some prizes. Can't imagine a better gilt than you've got there. Wait and see."

"Thanks, Dad. Hey?" I had to tell him. The knot in my stomach might twist the ability to breathe right out of my body.

"Yup?"

But I still couldn't say it. "When will you be back?"

"By chore time. I'll chore at home early and come back up to check on you—and see the horse show. Call if you think of anything we forgot."

I nodded.

Dad guided the truck and trailer back toward the road.

I sat, unable to quit thinking about the army of earthmovers and the hog factory moving in.

Gerbert and Herbert, the barrows, came nosing over to the toes of my tennis shoes. Helga, the gilt, flopped down where she could keep her beady little pig eyes on me. I had to admit, she was more than a little spoiled.

Dean's barrow, Buster, walked around and around and around, looking for a way out. He would have been happier in the same pen with the other three, but each exhibitor was supposed to have his or her own pen, so poor Buster was destined for a lonely week.

Pigs are amazingly smart. People don't know that if they've never known any pigs. I sat on the fence, thinking about creatures like these, who knew and loved me and trusted me—mostly because I fed them, but nevertheless, they loved me—being kept in a giant factory where their entire short, destined-for-pork lives would be confined to a space smaller than these 4-H fair pens, so small they could barely turn around. No fresh air or nosing in mud or jumping and squealing in play would ever be theirs. They would breathe, eat, sleep, drink, and poop in a tiny space until they were big enough to be cut up into pork chops and bacon. It made me sick.

These three buddies of mine would end up in the meat market. Even Helga, after she was done having some litters of piglets, would eventually be transformed into sausage. I had no illusions about that. But up until the point of sausage making, I would make sure her life was happy. These were animals for food and money, not pets. But, as Dad always taught me, they live so we can eat, so the least we can do is make their short lives of sacrifice as comfortable and pleasant as possible in appreciation. That's respect for life, he said. Sort of like the Indians, I always thought. I rubbed each of my pigs' bristly ears. They had finally all settled down for naps in the clean wood chip bedding. I gave Buster a pat, too, and then I headed out to see the fair.

The county fair smelled and sounded the way it had every summer for as long as I could remember; the mixture of animal smells—cattle, pigs, sheep, horses, chickens, and off-beat animals like goats and rabbits, with their distinct body and manure smells—all blended around their bleating, mooing, and neighing. Busy kids pitched out stalls, spread clean bedding, walked horses, and washed cattle in the sprayer area. The scents of hot dogs, hamburgers, and cotton candy drifted over it all and were inviting in spite of the tight knot in my stomach.

The Story County Fair had no midway. It was a 4-H fair, a farm kid's paradise, and everybody here came because they loved farming or some part of it. I walked, swinging my hands, drinking it in, past the snow cone booth by the show pavilion where I would show my pigs on Tuesday, and ran smack into the Thompson boys at the door of the dairy cattle barn.

"Got your porkers installed?" Hank asked.

"Yup. Your milk bags?"

The boys nodded.

I turned with them. We ambled around the grounds, talking, greeting other friends, soaking it in.

"Your camel jockey gonna come watch you show your pigs?" Hank finally asked.

"You bigot!" I punched him in the shoulder.

"Just wondered if a Muslim can attend a pork event, is all. You know I like Rafi. Everybody likes Rafi."

"He can't *eat* pork, you idiot. He can *look* at it. He's coming to watch me in the show, yes."

We reached the display area. Here some farm implement dealers brought displays of the newest tractors, innovative planters and attachments for combines, and information about farm programs, progressive ideas, and the like. On election years, the candidates used all the remaining available space to promote their own causes from every angle they could think to appear agriculturally minded. "Gordon Smith for Iowa," blazed in bright blue with red and white trim. "The man for Iowa's times." His movie-star-like face smiled down at them from a billboard-sized banner. Hard to miss. "Your future governor will be here at the story county fair, Sunday night at 6:00 P.M., prior to the 4-H horseshow," the sign read.

"Do you know who that is?" Hank asked.

"Of course. He's running for governor."

"He's Smith of Smithville Pork. Don't you know that? He wants to be governor, and he wants to put hog factories all over

Iowa. And our illustrious U.S. president endorses him."

I stared at Hank. "Are you serious?"

Hank nodded, staring at Smith's picture. "He's a big lawyer in Des Moines and bought into the hog factory business. Dad says he helped put so much campaign money in the politicians' pockets that the *first weeks they were in office,* they lifted the restrictions on hog factory waste so they can dump whatever they want, wherever they want, into whatever rivers they want . . . and they can force all of us little farmers out of business 'cause we can't compete, of course, with that kind of production for market."

"Are you serious?" My stomach knot twisted a notch tighter. "How'd you know that?"

"Dead serious. I read about it. Dad said, too. Found out from some environmental lobbyists at the Farm Bureau . . . but of course the media shushed it up. Like any other environmental scandals since they've been in office."

I stood rooted.

"Come on, Kerry," David said. "Let's go see the beef cattle."

"Wait, you guys." I couldn't keep quiet any longer. "Listen. Last night, Rafi and I got stuck on the mud road across from you."

"Aha!" Hank burst into laugher, then leered at me and raised his eyebrows. "Parking . . . ooh. We're getting serious. *Really* serious."

"Shut up!" I said. "Just shut up and listen." And I told them about the night before.

When I finished, Hank's and David's mouths hung open. "Why didn't we see anything?"

"They came about eleven thirty. Now that I think about it, I'll bet they timed this so everybody would be at the fair and not notice until it was too late."

We walked, oblivious to the fair smells and sounds, and hatched our plan. Then we separated, talking to every 4-H kid we saw, and I went to Gates Hall, where my friend Sally was setting up food and nutrition exhibits. I gave Sally the lowdown and asked her to tell everybody she could about the hog factory and Smith's appearance at six. She didn't think it would be a problem, and assured me that 4-H girls had a plethora of butcher paper and poster supplies—and there were plenty of big mouths among them, too.

At five forty-five, there were a few dozen people near Smith's booth. David, Hank, and I positioned ourselves at the front as soon as a crowd began to gather. At five fifty-nine, Mr. Gordon Smith and a couple black-suited men stepped out of a black Ford Expedition bearing SMITH FOR GOVERNOR signs. He checked a microphone, and at six, he said, "It's delightful to be here with you at the Story County 4-H Fair." The words weren't dead on the airwaves yet, when an army of senior 4-H kids swarmed from every nearby barn. In less than half a minute, there was a fence of homemade tagboard and butcher paper signs entirely encircling the booth. The color of Smith's face changed, but his pasted-on politician smile never wavered, even as he realized he was surrounded by "STOP THE HOG FACTORIES BEFORE THEY START"; "POLITICIANS TAKE NOTE: HOGS DON'T VOTE"; "HOGS ARE OUR LIVELIHOOD"; "HOGS DESERVE LIFE WHILE THEY'RE ALIVE"; "HOG FACTORIES STINK-POLLUTE"; "KEEP IOWA RIVERS CLEAN"; and "HOG FACTORIES STEAL OUR WAY OF LIFE."

"Well, well," he began again. "I'm delighted to see how involved Story County young people really are."

"What about the hog factories?" yelled Sally's brother Tim.

"I don't know why you're upset about hog factories. That issue was decided in March. Young ladies and gentlemen, that's a *dead* issue. There are greater issues at stake for us tonight. Iowa's economy rests on the fate of its agriculture. Our economy comes largely from corn, hogs—"

"If it's a dead issue, why are you building a hog factory across from my house?" yelled David.

Smith sputtered. Spit actually flew from his lips as he scrambled for words. "That would be a great misunderstanding," he crooned. "There was a decision that no hog factory in Story County—"

"You're *lying!*" The words were out of my mouth so fast and so loud, I heard them before I knew I was thinking them. It was like the twist in my stomach handsprung and shot the accusation at Mr. Smith.

The crowd sucked in a collective breath like a tractor sucking air into its carburetor. Everybody, *everybody*, was staring at me.

Among the everybody, I saw Dad and Mom and Grandma standing in the crowd, thirty people away from me, inside the wall of tagboard signs. And my knees started to shake.

Mr. Smith turned toward me, eyes dark and angry, but that smile still plastered on as smoothly as his plastered hair. The combination looked demented. "Lying? I'd say the young lady is grossly misinformed."

My mother's disapproval was sharp from across the crowd. And I knew it would only get worse before it got better.

But all of this, this life we all had, summer smells included, was too important for me to back down now. So I took a deep breath and yelled, "There is a Smithville hog confinement farm going up in Story County two miles from my house. Right now. Across from Harold Thompson's farm. You're lying!"

"How do you know?" one of the collective everybodies yelled.

"What *are* you talking about?" Smith said to me. His voice was slippery, slimy, smooth.

I yelled back at his plaster smile. "You *know* what I'm talking about! I saw the earthmovers come last night. I *saw* them. Right across from the Harvey Thompson farm!" Here I couldn't look at Mom or Dad. "And one of the drivers said they were making a foundation for a Smithville hog factory!"

The crowd exploded. Smith sputtered into the mike, something to the effect that he didn't need to be a part of such nonsense, but his attempts at quieting the crowd were like throwing a glass of water on a burning ditch. Pandemonium.

Bodies were smashed together, and the noise was deafening, but in the hubbub, I felt an arm around me. I turned to see Rafi's face beside me. He'd wedged through the crowd to my side.

"What are you doing here?" I yelled.

"Just came to see the fair," he yelled over the racket. "I felt bad about last night, so I came to see you. I'm *proud* of you," he yelled into my ear. I hugged him. And together with my boyfriend who couldn't eat pork, I joined the chant, "Hog farms stink-pollute. Hog Farms stink-pollute."

In the hubbub, Gordon Smith was whisked away by the guys in black suits, shoving through the fence of posterboard. The chants grew in intensity but faded out as the black limo pulled away.

I leaned against Rafi and heaved a sigh. "We lost, didn't we? We can't win this fight. They're building no matter what."

He nodded against the top of my head. "I wish it weren't true," he said, and he held me tight.

The hog factory would go up, in spite of all our protests. Money talked louder than the whole county could chant. But at least, the truth was in the open. Maybe tomorrow, all this would be in the papers, and maybe Gordon Smith wouldn't be elected governor.

We turned, the two of us arm in arm, and found ourselves face-to-face with my parents' and grandmother's eyes. Over their heads above the fairgrounds, a pale moon had risen. I looked for Mars, the war god star, but it wasn't out yet.

"If you two are *just friends,* I'll eat my hat," Grandma said. Her pale blue eyes were flashing. "It's a sin, you know. A sin."

Dad's eyes were proud, but Mom's eyes were daggers of anger and accusation. *"Last night?"* she almost hissed.

I kept my arm in Rafi's and looked each of them straight in the eyes. "Listen," I said, "the sin would be not telling the truth. The truth is like this . . . "

LAUNCHPAD TO NEPTUNE

by Sara Ryan and Randy Powell

S. The hardest decision the day I was going to meet Gavin: what to wear. "Your prom dress, of course, sweetie," said Dean. "Shut up," I said. Then I said the hell with it and wore what I always wear these days. It didn't matter.

G. For the past half hour I've been sitting at a little table in the corner, drinking an iced latte with a double shot of espresso. It's noisy and crowded in here, lots of local oddballs and freaks, mostly college age. Not the place I would have chosen for our big reunion, but it's where Stephanie picked, so here I am.

I find the restroom, push open the door with the funky rooster symbol on it (at least I *think* it's a damn rooster and not a hen), and am hit with the smell of recent cigarette smoke. Somebody's at the urinal, so I head for the toilet stall, flip up the seat, shake hands with my best bud again, and take aim on a lone cigarette butt floating in the bowl. I jet-stream the butt around in circles, flip it a couple of times, then make it do a dizzying counterclockwise spin.

When I was nine years old, I thought this might be my calling in life—giving peeing performances. My parents were always telling me how everybody has a calling, something they're truly gifted at. My dad's gift was bootlicking and ass-wiping top-level corporate executives. Mom's was using the exercise machines at the health club and giving luncheons. My gift was doing acrobatic peeing tricks and target shooting. I figured it would be a great calling; I'd get to drink all the Coke and Pepsi I wanted.

And these days I drink plenty of Coke and Pepsi. And a shitload of iced lattes. It keeps me buzzed and revved now that I've been trying to stay off booze and pot so I can pass my mandatory monthly drug test and get off probation. And my life's calling, what I do for a living? Bus tables at a Chinese restaurant in downtown Seattle.

Tonight, however, is my night off, and I am trying to sink a cigarette butt in a toilet bowl in the restroom of the Last Exit in one of the raunchier neighborhoods in the heart of the Latte Belt, and waiting for Stephanie Jones.

Who I often think of when I pee.

She used to watch me pee in the woods behind her playhouse. She was a great audience; so *impressed*.

That playhouse—man, that's what impressed me. Her father and her big brother, Peter the dildo, had built it. It had nooks and niches and hidden escape passages into the woods, and you had to climb a rope ladder to get in, where it smelled like fresh cedar and you could hear the rain tapping on the roof.

Yeah, I was jealous. Stephanie and I were the same age, and she seemed to get everything she wanted—or at least everything I wanted. And there wasn't anything she wasn't good at. Same with Peter the dildo. My parents were constantly reminding me of it— why can't you just *try* to be more like Stephanie and Peter? Peter and Stephanie are always doing some interesting project, such good kids, so bright and active.

But I didn't feel inferior when I pulled down my pants in front of her and performed impressive peeing stunts.

She asked me if I'd ever been in a pissing contest. "Sure, lots of them," I said, having no idea what she meant.

When I turned twelve, I started having fantasies of kissing her inside her playhouse. Other places, too.

I finish peeing and stop at the sink to wash my hands, a sanitary habit I've gotten into while working at the Asian Buffet. I check out the mirror, just to see what I look like—what Stephanie will see when she shows up. Sure enough, what I look like is an eighteen-year-old busboy.

I'm still amazed she wanted to see me at all, considering the fact that we haven't seen each other for two years, since eleventh grade. And the last couple times we saw each other were not good.

How this reunion came about is that a few months ago, a friend of mine got me a one-night job as a valet parking attendant at some gala charity event at the museum. All these luxury cars rolling up and dumping off old people in their gowns and tuxes, and one of the couples turns out to be Mr. and Mrs.

Jones—Stephanie's parents. Opening the door for his wife, Charlie Jones didn't give me enough of a glance to recognize me. But Dolly, all decked out in her jewels and evening gown and suntan, shoots me a double take. And then screams.

"Gavin? My goodness, it *is* you! Charlie, look! It's Gavin!"

"Well, what do you know! Gavin, old boy! How are you!"

They marveled at how much I had grown. They asked what I was up to these days. They showed phony delight at hearing that I'd graduated from high school. They forced their smiles to stay propped up when I told them I was living in a rented room in a house. They didn't seem surprised when I told them that my parents and little sister had moved to Texas and started a new life.

I was polite, but I had never liked Charlie or Dolly Jones.

I asked how their kids were doing.

Quite well, quite well, they said. Peter was at Harvard or MIT or somewhere; Kaylie had made the Junior Nationals in whatever the hell thing she was into—ice skating or gymnastic dancing or baton twirling.

They didn't say anything about Stephanie. Zero. Mr. Jones glanced at his watch, then at his wife.

I had nothing to lose, so I came out with it. "How's Stephanie?" And waited for them to tell me she was doing just splendidly in her first year at such and such college.

But they both gave me these empty, almost helpless stares, their faces turning a shade of pale, and I braced myself for some horrible piece of news.

Finally Mrs. Jones put her tanned hand on my arm and flashed that phony church smile that I'd seen so many times, and drew close to me so I could smell her perfume and breath-mint breath, and said, "Gavin I'm so *glad* things are finally working out for your parents. Give them our best!" And she turned and linked arms with her husband, and they walked up the museum steps, and I parked their car.

For days after that, I couldn't stop thinking about their faces when I'd asked about Stephanie. What was the deal? Why hadn't they told me anything?

Not knowing what I hoped to find, I spent about five hours doing Google searches on my computer. A zillion hits came up for Stephanie Jones. My heart was slamming as I scrolled through the obituaries first, but they were all different Stephanie Joneses.

Then I hit a lot of stuff about her high school activities. We'd gone to the same schools together right up until spring of eleventh grade, when my parents moved out to the suburbs and I went with them. But we'd always traveled in different universes. She took all the high-achiever classes. She hung out with sensitive, egghead types, while I hung out with guys who tried to see who could fart the loudest. If it hadn't been for our parents' connection, Stephanie would never have known I existed.

And now I was trying to find out if *she* still existed. Her name came up in some old newsletter, at least two years old, that mentioned she was doing some community service project. It gave her e-mail address. A defunct address, no doubt, but what the hell, I figured I'd drop her a note and see if anything came back.

8. "Jesus Christ," I said, startling the person next to me at the scruffy little Internet café. I grabbed my coffee and took a long

gulp while I looked again at the screen. Yeah, that really was Gavin's name in my inbox. He said hi. He'd just run across my e-mail totally by accident. He wanted to know how it was going.

I'd been meaning to change my address, but I was glad I hadn't yet. Glad, with a fast heartbeat and sweat suddenly slicking my forehead, my hands, the space between my nose and mouth. I typed a reply, suggesting that we get together, and hit send before I could think.

I walked out of the café without logging out or paying, and down the street to my pal Dean's apartment, where I switched from stimulant to depressant and kicked myself for answering the e-mail. Dean said not to be so upset, it was great to have the chance to reconnect with someone from my past; it was an important thing to do. I had a lot of balls. That made us laugh.

The first time we met, we were babies. Gavin's mom used to have this picture of the two of us lying on a blanket, both half asleep, with those squinty expressions babies get, our tiny fists clenched. We look so much alike.

When we were six, Gavin marked me for life.

It seems odd when I look back on it that we were together so much as kids. I think it was mostly due to my dad. He not only loves being important, he loves seeing himself as family friendly. So every time he wanted to get his core staff together, he'd bring them all to our place and encourage them to bring spouses and kids.

Anyway, Gavin and I had run into the woods to hide from this whiny girl who was always trying to follow us around. I can't remember which of us got the idea to pick up branches off the ground and use them as swords, but I remember the fight. We were laughing and shouting when we started, but then it turned serious and deliberate.

I was trying to convince myself that we really were dueling knights, concentrating so hard, trying to turn the clacking of sticks into the clang of metal on metal, that I didn't see it coming when Gavin stabbed me in the eye. There was just the sudden surprise of the pain and the red cloud over the vision in my right eye. We both screamed and then went running back to the lawn where the adults were gathered.

Gavin had dropped his branch, but I still had mine. This will sound weird, but I really wish someone had taken a picture of me then: standing there with my bloody eye, holding my branch in both hands as though I was waiting for another attack.

Mom said they had the worst time getting me to let go of it.

Gavin got into a lot of trouble. His mom was hysterical.

I got to ride in an ambulance and wear a cool patch that I refused to give up after my eye healed, because I'd decided it made me a pirate.

But Gavin wouldn't play with me for a long time after that, and I spent countless bleak afternoons with the whiny girl. She liked to play dress-up, so every time we were at my house, I'd give her clothes. Until my mom caught on, I was doing a great job of divesting myself of all the froufiest items in my closet.

Whiny Girl also had a huge, horrible doll collection. I had dolls, too, and I liked them a lot, but I wouldn't share them with her. My dolls fought crime. Hers had tea parties.

The one good time I had with her was when I convinced her that we needed to hold gymnastics trials for the doll Olympics.

"Time for the long jump!" I remember saying. Then I

hurled the doll as far as I could. She wailed, and I couldn't stop laughing.

But now, laughing was the furthest thing from my mind. Why was I even here? It was such a dumb-ass idea. I rubbed my chin, chewed my lip, looked at the clock. It was a while before Gavin was supposed to arrive; I could still duck out. Or I could use the john. I got up, walked across the room, grimaced at the cheesy restroom signs (one featured a rooster, the other a fluffy chick), and pushed open the door.

I used to have this playhouse. "Playhouse," Dad called it, but it was bigger than my current apartment. Gavin and I used to spend a lot of time there, I guess until we were about ten. There wasn't much inside, except for my collection. Every time my family went to the beach, which was fairly often, I'd pick up things that had washed up onshore. Mom discouraged me from keeping entire bottles, but bits of glass were okay, as long as their edges had been dulled by water and sand. I'd put the glass in my pockets so my hands would be free for other finds: smooth stones, sand dollars, bleached and gnarled driftwood.

Once I'd taken the stuff back home and put it inside the playhouse, it never looked or felt right. But somehow I could never remember that when I was on the beach. I always thought, with each new salt-crusted object I gathered, that the whole collection would take on meaning.

It never did, for me, but Gavin always seemed fascinated. He'd trace the patterns on a sand dollar, or pick up one of the pieces of driftwood as though it was a baseball bat and swing it, listening to the way it whistled in the air.

Gavin paid attention to my collection. I concentrated on him. I used to ask him to do things, things it embarrasses me, now, to remember. And I was so matter-of-fact about my requests. I didn't think of them as weird, yet.

At school, once we got to junior high, Gavin and I didn't really talk to each other. We were always in different classes. Oh, sure, if we saw each other in the halls, we'd nod, but he always seemed to be surrounded by the kind of people I had no idea how to talk to. Actually, that was most people.

We'd still hang out at Dad's corporate shindigs, though.

But when we were sixteen, everything got messed up. Gavin and I were both suffering, innocent bystanders at the latest Dad-stravaganza. This time, he had the Team (he called them the Team that year; next year, it was the Workgroup—the year after that, he laid them all off) at a ski lodge. It was summer, so skiing itself was not an option, but we were close to the ocean, and there were woods, and the lodge, of course, had a pool and a hot tub.

The Team, when not pursuing healthful outdoor exercise, was trust building and brainstorming, furiously engaged in process improvement. The dozen or so Team Kids, ranging in age from precocious eleven to over-it-all eighteen, were sizing each other up, seeing who would deflate under the onslaught of our casual, bored mockery. We'd already demolished all of our parents, those ridiculously easy targets, and had moved on to each other: who was a virgin, who hadn't been drunk, who didn't swear enough, whose clothes were the wrong brands. I was the first three. Gavin was the last.

Gavin and I started avoiding the rest of the Team Kids. We did this with no conscious strategy or discussion, it just happened, without words, the two of us detaching from the group and spending more and more time by ourselves.

I was aware, on some level, that this time I was spending with Gavin meant something different to him than it did to me. But since I couldn't articulate what it meant to me, I ignored the awareness.

G. Back at my little table, sipping another iced latte, for some reason I'm thinking of the ski lodge. Not one of my finest moments. I remember those stupid Team Kids. All their yak yakking about their ski trips and ski equipment and multiple orgasms and designer clothing labels. The endless gossiping and giggling. And all that campy lodge shit—the beach, the pool, the going out on the lake in a rowboat. The fucking mosquitos.

I just wanted to sit in the lounge unbothered, sucking up Cokes and cable TV. But I knew how important this retreat was to my parents. My dad had been getting a lot of pressure from old Charlie Jones, and he needed to score some brownie points in a big way—so I had to at least try to fit in and participate. That was back in the days when I still did try, occasionally.

Stephanie was a bundle of energy at that lodge. She did everything. She was into all that outdoor crap. Maybe she felt sorry for me and started spending time with me out of politeness.

The days of my impressing her with peeing tricks were long gone. So were the days of the playhouse and admiring her collection of washed-up beach debris. When we became teenagers, I started feeling self-conscious around her, kind of like I had to keep checking my fly to make sure it was zipped up.

But over the years I'd still had visions of kissing her. I liked looking at her when I saw her at school or family get-togethers. Occasionally I had a feeling she was looking at me, too.

At the lodge, we kept finding ourselves alone together. It just kept happening without much effort. It was hard for me to believe, but I felt like I was getting some definite vibes of encouragement from her.

I started thinking about making a move on her. I'd never done anything with a girl before, and I thought Stephanie and that lodge would be a good place to start. A little practice wouldn't do either one of us any permanent damage, right?

We sat by the fire. She didn't seem to mind sitting by me. I noticed she chewed on her lips a lot. She kept applying lip balm. I wanted to have a chew on her lips too.

We went for a hike one afternoon when all the other perfect kids were doing something extremely wholesome like playing volleyball or bragging about how many times they'd had sex in a hot tub. We followed a trail that led away from the beach and went up through dense forest. It was all uphill. After ten or fifteen minutes, we reached the top of the bluff. I felt like my gut was going to split, I'm huffing and puffing and sweating. Stephanie was hardly out of breath.

We found a small clearing surrounded by trees, sheltered from the wind from the ocean. It was peaceful and shady in there. The air was still. Totally private and secluded.

We sat down on the soft, dry grass, our backs resting against a log. We looked out through the trees at the ocean.

"What is this place?" I said. "A launchpad to Neptune?"

She looked at me and laughed. "Yeah, I like that."

Then she said, "I'd like to come back here someday. I'd sit up here all night, by myself."

"Why would you do that?"

"Well, during the day I'd sit here. I'd sit very still. First I'd get bored and restless, but pretty soon I'd start seeing things—an eagle, a deer, maybe even a bear. And then night would come. I'd be scared at first, and homesick and lonely. But then I'd sort of get swallowed up, lose myself in the darkness. Blend in with everything. The fear and loneliness would go away. The stars would come out. I'd hear things and see visions. I'd see myself. I'd see *into* myself."

Wow. I just stared at her. Her eyes seemed so deep, and there was something in them, in her, I'd never seen before, but I didn't know what it was. "I'd sign up for that," I said in a quiet voice. And I meant it. Come up here and catch a glimpse of something inside myself.

It wasn't until we were hiking back down to the lodge that I realized I'd missed the perfect chance to kiss her. The chance would never come again. Tomorrow we were packing up and leaving. I felt a kind of panic.

8. The last night of the retreat, there was a banquet. You'd think, since we were at a ski lodge, we'd just have the banquet at the lodge's own restaurant. But that was too mundane for Dad. His great scheme, which he thought was amusing, was to pay homage to his early days as a go-getting entrepreneur. He worked so many hours back then, that he'd never be home for dinner. Instead, he'd get cheap Chinese food delivered to his office. But actually serving cheap Chinese food to his employees would be déclassé. So he hired a master chef to cater this enormous, formal, multi-course banquet and decorate the whole lodge to look like a cheap Chinese restaurant. The red lamps, the bright gold dragons, the plastic, patterned dinnerware, and even the place mats, which

I recognized as a remarkably dumbed-down-for-white-devils look at Chinese astrology. The Team Kids had spent most of the banquet trying to get served alcohol, but the catering staff knew who was paying them and refused.

"Hey, Stephanie, what year were you born?" Christina, the oldest Team Kid, suddenly asked. I told her, and she screeched, "Oh, my God, that's so funny! Look, everybody: Stephanie was born in the Year of the Cock!"

Next to the picture of the rooster on the place mat, I read "A pioneer in spirit, you are devoted to work and quest after knowledge. You are selfish and eccentric. Rabbits are trouble. Snakes and Oxen are fine."

I knew it was just a cutesy place mat, designed to spark witty conversation at a restaurant, and I knew Christina wanted to embarrass me, but I actually liked the description. I definitely was devoted to work, and I quested after knowledge, too. We were so rich it was practically a given that I was selfish, and as for eccentric, well, yeah. I looked at the birth years listed for the other signs mentioned. Christina was a Rabbit. So was my dad. Gavin was an Ox.

"I was born then," Gavin said. Why was he lying?

Christina looked at him with one eyebrow raised. "So, you're big on cock, too, I take it?"

Gavin flushed, and I was furious. I was about to say something, I didn't know what, when he said, "That's right, I've got a big cock, and you can suck it. That *is* what you said, right?"

He didn't wait for her to answer, just got up from the table and left. Christina was only fazed for a few seconds. She laughed a little laugh and said, "Well, I guess we know what *he's* insecure about."

I scowled, but I said nothing. Anything I said would get me into trouble. So I waited till the end of dinner to excuse myself.

I went back to my room and changed. I didn't exactly set out to go looking for Gavin. It just so happened that the place he'd gone was where I ended up: the pool. We swam for a while. Then I was cold, so I moved to the hot tub. Back then, it seemed like I was always either too cold or too hot.

Gavin got in. I remember the splash sounded especially loud, and I wondered about echoes and water and tiled walls. After he got in, we were quiet. I wanted to say something about what a bitch Christina was, but instead I said, "You picked a good time to leave dinner—the dessert was even lamer than the rest of it."

On the word *it*, Gavin kissed me.

Was I surprised? Yes, no.

Did I like it? Yes, no.

It was too much, somehow. I pushed him away, got out of the pool, went back to my room, not thinking anything coherent.

It was the last night of the retreat.

I saw him a few weeks later, but he ignored me.

I didn't try talking to him again after that, and before long, I stopped seeing him around. I heard that he'd moved, but I didn't know where, and I had no one to ask.

G. I finish my second iced latte. No sign of Stephanie anywhere. I'd better take another leak before she gets here.

This time I use the urinal.

I wish I hadn't started thinking about that damn ski lodge. It always makes me burn with shame. How many times have I wished I could go back and undo it?

I remember I was in the pool, still shaking from some stupid remark I'd made to one of the other girls, but Stephanie showed up and I stopped shaking in a hurry. She looked damn good in that bikini. Kind of flat-chested but nice legs, really nice butt, long sleek arms and neck. She seemed to keep on kind of swimming past me, near to me, like a fish, grazing me with her wake. When she got out of the pool and walked over to the hot tub, my blood was popping. Why did I grab her so suddenly? Why did I mash my face into her mouth, tasting lip balm and chlorine and fortune cookie? What could I possibly have been thinking? She'd been utterly astonished and dumbfounded and grossed out. So grossed out.

I should have told her that I cared about her or something. But all I could think about was pouncing on her and getting in some practice. At the time I didn't even realize it: She's the only girl I've ever cared about.

After that, I was so embarrassed and ashamed I couldn't even be in the same room with her. My pride and confidence were gone—kaput.

But that's not the worst moment of my life.

There was one more time after that. A few weeks later, a week before the start of eleventh grade. A balmy Sunday evening, my friend and I were riding our bikes around, just enjoying one of the last days of summer. And suddenly there was Stephanie, zipping by me in this hot-looking white convertible. She saw me, and I saw her. She pulled over to the curb up ahead, opened her door, faced me, waited for me to ride up to her on my bike. She was sitting there smiling awkwardly, her face red and flushed, and when I approached on my bike, I heard her clear her throat and say, "Gavin, I haven't seen you for a while and I just wanted to—"

I kept on riding past her. My friend said, "Hey, Gavin, that girl was trying to—" But I ignored him too, I just kept riding.

That's the worst moment of my life.

If I could go back, I'd go to that place in the woods, that clearing at the top of the bluff where she told me she'd stay up all night.

I wonder if she ever did that? I wonder if she heard things and saw visions?

My life went steadily downhill after that hot-tub incident. My mom and dad had been going deep in debt, trying to keep up with the Charlie and Dolly Jones lifestyle. But Dad never did score enough brownie points, and old Charlie fired him just after Christmas. My folks were bankrupt. We sold our house and moved to a cheap apartment way out in the boonies, and I started a new school in the spring of my junior year. By then I had stopped trying altogether—trying to be a good son, good student, good whatever. I chased after new visions with the help of various chemicals, got in some trouble during my senior year, got busted a couple times for stupid things, but somehow managed to eventually graduate. Meanwhile my dad couldn't find a decent job anywhere in the Northwest, so one day my mom and dad and little sister decided to move to Texas, a brand-new life in a new city with a new opportunity. I decided not to go with them. What would be the point? I was on probation with a suspended sentence—still am, actually. I moved back to Seattle, got a job, rented a cheap room.

Some skinny guy is leaning against the sink staring into the mirror. He's got a lame attempt going at a beard and mustache. I didn't notice him come into the restroom.

He's looking into the mirror, not at himself, but at me.

There's something in his cheekbones and in his eyes that causes a little prickly feeling in the center of my chest.

"Hey, Gavin," he says cautiously.

I step away from the urinal with my fly gaping.

I open my mouth, about to say something like *Do I know you?*

"It's good to see you," the guy says, half facing me.

I'm frozen for another moment. Then I walk past him, out the door into the crowded coffee shop. I stop and lean my forehead against the wall. My knees are shaky. I notice my fly is still open.

This is a nightmare. I'm having trouble breathing. My forehead is stuck to the wall. I should have said something—but what? How about "hello"? Or "hey, long time, no see ... *fella*"? Christ, it's like a repeat of that last time I was on my bike. You gutless piece of shit. I can't go back in that restroom. And he doesn't seem to be coming out. Or she.

I am a coward, but that's okay, I'll live with it, I won't go back in that restroom with him in there. Or her. Too weird. She had hair—*on her face!* An attempt at a beard and mustache. I was not imagining that. Maybe it's a joke? Did she decide to dress up in a costume and surprise me in the men's room? Why is she still in there? Is she waiting for me? Does she just stand at sinks waiting for people so she can shock the hell out of them? I can't go in there. I would look really stupid if I walked back in there. Why did you walk out? You gutless ... okay. Okay, I'll go back in. Jesus.

This is so typical. The one girl I ever cared about does not appear to be a girl anymore.

S. Of course he was in the men's room, the room I still have to psych myself up to walk into, every single time.

And now he won't come back.

Sometimes I found myself thinking that when Gavin poked that stick in my eye, it went all the way into my brain and shoved everything off-kilter. I used to read books where the hero would talk about feeling different, but it always turned out to be such a bullshit kind of different. You know, like everyone expects him to be a football player but really he wants to wear black and write political songs. Oh, cry me a goddamn river. I gave up reading novels after one too many of those stories where the guy discovers his True Self with the help of his Sensitive Art Teacher, or his mom's No-Nonsense New Husband, or That Girl He Always Thought Was Weird. I decided I'd only read things that were true.

When I took my driver's test, there was a point when I was supposed to make a left turn, but I misjudged the timing. So I got caught between lanes, with the car at an awkward angle. Everyone around me was honking. I knew I was blocking traffic, but there was no room for me to move.

I sat, panicked, clutching the steering wheel, waiting for the light to change, waiting for someone to make a space for me, and suddenly I started laughing, with a crazy edge, because the sick feeling in the pit of my stomach was so familiar. There was nothing at all new to me about being trapped.

Supposedly, animals gnaw their own legs off to escape from traps.

When I got my license, Dad bought me a brand-new flashy little white convertible. After a decent interval had passed, I traded it for a truck that was a few years old and got the difference in cash. Then I went on my first road trip.

I didn't start out with a firm plan. All I knew was that I wanted to escape. But before long, I knew exactly where I was going. It kind of surprised me that I was able to find it again so easily, but I've always been a good navigator.

I didn't want to stay in the lodge itself, figuring it would probably be full of people who would remind me of Dad and his colleagues, but I remembered that you could set up camp in the woods. So I drove up to the ranger station. It was a sunny day. I was wearing sunglasses and a cap to cut the glare.

"Hey, buddy," the ranger said. "Need a camping permit?"

I cleared my throat. "Yeah," I said, deepening my voice.

"Six bucks."

I gave him six bucks.

"Enjoy your weekend, buddy."

Did I tip my cap in acknowledgment? Or did I just nod? I don't know.

Anyway, it was right where I remembered: the small clearing, surrounded by trees, sheltered from the wind. I didn't bother with a tent, just unrolled my sleeping bag on the ground.

When I'd told Gavin I wanted to see into myself, it was sort of a lie. I knew who I was. I'd always known. What I wanted was to see if there was some way I could reconcile the person I knew I was with the person I was expected to be.

I didn't see any animals that night. I heard leaves rustling, branches snapping. And a couple of times, I thought I glimpsed shining eyes.

I did see the stars. They were so bright they seemed harsh, as though I could have gone blind from looking at them, like staring at the sun during an eclipse.

So many more stars than you can see in the city. So clear.

It was clear, too, what I had to do when I left. Not easy. God, the furthest from easy. But clear.

I moved out before I could get kicked out, drained my college fund, and paid exorbitant amounts of money for the privilege of having endless, exhausting conversations with well-meaning professionals who wanted to ascertain the nature of my disorder, which I didn't consider a disorder. It was just that sense of wrongness, that feeling of being stuck between lanes, that was always there. I wanted to address it in a way that seemed logical to me.

I prefer understatement to hyperbole, so I'll just say that it's all been a hassle. Peter will send the occasional e-mail—he likes political forwards—and Kaylie chats with me online sometimes, late at night after all her friends have gone to sleep. But Mom and Dad? No, they don't talk to me. Ever. Kaylie says they pretend I don't exist, and really, the person they wanted me to be doesn't anymore, so maybe they're right.

G. I push the door open, making sure it's the one with the rooster on it.

She . . . he . . . is still standing by the sink. He looks at me.

"Sorry I shocked you, Gavin."

"You didn't shock me. So, what's new? What have you been up to anyway? Played any miniature golf lately?"

She laughs and shakes her head.

"How about that collection of yours?" I ask. "You still have your collection?"

"What collection?"

"Uh, it was a bunch of washed-up beach stuff. You kept it in your playhouse in the backyard. Do you still have the collection? Do you still have the playhouse?"

"No," Stephanie says.

In this restroom, leaning against the sink with his legs stretched out in front of him, he seems to have achieved a level of casualness and calmness that is far superior to mine.

I force myself to look at her face.

I say, "D-did you—ah—"

"Hm?" She is looking at me attentively, waiting.

"Did you ... get some kind of, ahhh, sex ... alteration ... ?"

She chews on her upper lip, just like always.

"I go by Stephen now."

"Stephen?"

"Yeah."

"I suppose you"—I swallow—"have some reason for ... ?"

He leans toward me, as if he's going to make a move on me. "Reason?"

"Hey, listen," I say, putting up my hands, "I just want to say ... I'm sorry about what happened in the—"

The door opens, and a middle-aged man comes walking in. He gives us a glance and goes over to the urinal and starts doing his thing.

"What happened in the what?" Stephen says.

I lower my voice. "Hot tub."

Stephen looks at me for a moment. "You mean when you started—"

"Yeah," I interrupt.

The guy at the urinal starts whistling quietly.

"You didn't do anything bad," Stephen says. "You just—you just started kissing me, that's all. I wasn't expecting it—it took me by surprise. How come you ignored me after that? I figured you hated me."

"I was pretty embarrassed about it," I say. "I thought you hated me."

After the guy finally flushes and walks out, giving us another glance and not stopping to wash his hands, I say to Stephen, "The last time I saw you, when I just ignored you . . . that's been driving me crazy."

"When you rode past me, I kept thinking you'd turn around and come back," Stephen says. "I waited. Same as tonight."

"I just have to ask you something," I say. "Does this—does your *change*—it doesn't have anything to do with what happened in the hot tub, does it?"

Stephen stares at me. He blinks. His face looks like it's about to break into a smile. "Now, let me get this straight. You're asking me if I did a complete change of identity, including changing my name and taking hormone shots for the last six months, all because of your kissing me three years ago in a hot tub?"

"Well, it did seem like you were pretty grossed out at the time."

"Not *that* grossed out."

"That's a relief," Gavin says. "I wouldn't want to be responsible."

Mentioning the hormones, that was like jumping off a cliff—or taking off from that launchpad to Neptune. I find myself smiling, saying, "I didn't say you weren't responsible."

"Now, wait a minute here—"

"I just said it didn't have anything to do with the hot tub."

Gavin looks ill. "I'm not following you."

"Yeah, well,"—I continue my launch—"I've been following you, in a way. I've been watching you all my life. Studying you."

Gavin's face is breaking out into a sweat. "Why would you do that?"

It's funny how the words come, so easily. I'm not just explaining to him, I'm explaining to myself. Telling the truth again, but one I've never discussed, not even with the well-meaning professionals, because I've only just now figured it out.

"Because, you dope, I've always admired you. You're the one person in the world I always wanted to be like. So I watched everything: the way you walked, the way you acted. Yeah, even the way you peed. And somehow when I did, I started to catch little glimpses of myself. You were really kind of like my guide. And I'm glad I finally have a chance to tell you that."

Glad, I say, and I am, but also terrified. This beats out the facial hair for bizarre, I'm certain, and maybe in another minute he'll bolt again, or hit me, or worse, but I stand, or rather lean, my ground.

I am holding on to the sink—holding on as my shithouse universe swirls and tilts, as if I am the cigarette butt in the toilet bowl and somebody has flushed the toilet and launched me spinning and spinning on my way down. I need to sit. I need to sit and think about what Stephen has just told me. When I do sit down on the floor next to the sink, I notice my fly is still open. I reach down and zip it up.

AUTHORS & INSPIRATION

Chris Crutcher, a former family therapist and mental health consultant in the Pacific Northwest, brings humor and unflinching realism to his coming-of-age fiction. That combination of comedy and tragedy has made his work a staple in the world of young adult literature, with an adult following nearly as strong as his teen base. "It's universal," he says. "It's about human connection, and it's about telling the truth." In eleven novels, including *Staying Fat for Sarah Byrnes, Whale Talk,* and *Deadline;* two short story collections; and *King of the Mild Frontier: An Ill-Advised Autobiography,* Crutcher's devotion to honesty has raised the hackles of censors across the United States—but he is never fearful of controversy. Being named the 1998 recipient of the NCTE's National Intellectual Freedom Award is among his proudest achievements. "Intellectual freedom is not something we should need awards for," he says. "It is simply the freedom to hold and express our ideas; the freedom to stand for who we are and what we believe. It is a birthright."
www.chriscrutcher.com

CRUTCHER'S INSPIRATION

Most teenagers claim not to "get" what makes the other person tick in a relationship. What most don't "get" is what makes *them* tick. The history one brings into a relationship—the personality structure—may be the single most important factor in predicting the outcome.

Kelly Milner Halls has been a freelance journalist and children's author for nearly twenty years, with twenty books for young readers (including *Albino Animals, Tales of the Cryptids, Saving the Baghdad Zoo*, and *In Search of Sasquatch*), and more than 1,600 articles and book reviews published in magazines and newspapers, including *Teen People, VOYA, Book Links, Booklist, Guidepost for Teens, Parenting Teens, Writer's Digest*, the *Chicago Tribune*, the *Washington Post*, the *Denver Post*, and dozens of others. After more than a decade of writing about literature, she moved to Spokane, Washington, and is studying with Spokane residents Chris Crutcher, Terry Davis, and Terry Trueman to learn the craft of fiction. This is her debut YA effort, but she hopes others will soon follow. She's raised two young adults—Kerry, 28, and Vanessa, 21—on her own as a single parent. *www.kellymilnerhalls.com*

MILNER HALLS'S INSPIRATION

Like all good students, I followed the lead of my mentor when it came to the core direction of the stories we wrote. But once introduced to the spirit of Wanda Wickham, she took on a literary life of her own. Her pathos belongs to Chris; her voice was a joy all my own. It was an honor to team with the Stotan, and a learning experience I wouldn't trade.

Joseph Bruchac lives with his wife in the New York Adirondack foothills in the house where his grandparents raised him. Heralded for his moving, lyrical fiction, including *Dawn Land*, *Skeleton Man*, and *Wabi: A Hero's Tale*, he is often inspired by his Abenaki tribal ancestry and regularly performs traditional Abenaki music to help keep that ancient energy alive. With more than seventy published books to his credit, Bruchac has been awarded dozens of literary honors, including a Rockefeller Humanities Fellowship, a National Endowment for the Arts Writing Fellowship for Poetry, and the Cherokee Nation Prose Award. *www.josephbruchac.com*

BRUCHAC'S INSPIRATION

I should mention a couple of things that inspired my storytelling. One, which is more background than main story, is my own involvement over the last thirty years in the martial arts. Another is the importance of recognizing we can never fully know who someone is just by their outward appearance. The third is Indian basketball. Most non-Indians have no idea how important it is to Native people. The young men and women who play basketball are the warriors of today in many of our communities.

Cynthia Leitich Smith, a proud member of the Muscogee (Creek) Tribe, spins her artful tales, often with a Native American flavor, from the warm expanses of the Lone Star State, in Austin, Texas. From picture books like *Jingle Dancer*, to middle-grade fiction including *Indian Shoes*, to young adult literature like *Tantalize*, her signature approach assures thoughtful, heartfelt storytelling, regardless of her target age group. Each of her books has been critically acclaimed, and her short stories have appeared in several other anthologies. Paired with her idol, Joseph Bruchac, Smith helped create strong, modern characters unquestionably proud of their ancestral past.

www.cynthialeitichsmith.com

SMITH'S INSPIRATION

I'd never write "big strapping hero meets petite, helpless princess." I mean, really . . . yawn. So what a treat it was to read Joe's tale of two heroes—Bobby and Nancy—whose looks and attitude flip outdated gender stereotypes. It made me wonder about these outward opposites, inner soul mates. What could they become to each other? So that's the story I wrote.

James Howe may be best known for rabbit vampires—the famed Bunnicula—but his expertise extends far beyond chapter-book fame. He's been an actor and a model. He's written picture books and young adult novels, many, including *The Misfits*, *The Watcher*, and *Totally Joe*, critically acclaimed for their courageous portrayals of outsiders drawn together by their humanity and their will to survive. From his home just outside of New York City, Howe has gathered awards as a writer, an educator, and a public speaker. His Internet inspired submission in this anthology is deserving of a few more. But he has yet to create his own cyber presence—he has no website.

HOWE'S INSPIRATION

The Internet is one of the most common places people meet these days, yet it is not even a place. It is a zone of mystery, possibility, and danger, which at its best offers the chance to find oneself by finding kindred souls. For some people, especially those who, in Thoreau's words, "live lives of quiet desperation," it can be a lifeline.

I live just north of New York City and often travel on a road that winds north and west upstate. It is a road dotted with small towns in isolated, rural areas. I stop along the way to eat in diners much like the one in this story. I've often wondered about the lives of the people in these towns. What would it be like, I asked myself as this story began to take shape in my head, to be a gay teenage boy growing up in one of these towns, where most men and boys hunt and fish and the culture is predominantly macho? How would someone so different survive? The Internet was the lifeline I threw to one such boy to find out what one answer might be.

Ellen Wittlinger was a librarian in another life—no, make that another phase of this action-filled lifetime. Offering books and young readers safe harbor, she learned firsthand about the magical ability of literature to change already transitional teen lives. So perhaps it was fated that she win one of the American Library Association's Printz Honor designations in the year 2000 for her very first young adult book, *Hard Love*. Although other books came before, including *Lombardo's Law*, and have come after, including *ZigZag* and *Parrotfish*, the tenderness and warmth of Wittlinger's fiction has remained consistent. It flashes with brilliance in the unforgettable story pair created with Jim Howe. *www.ellenwittlinger.com*

WITTLINGER'S INSPIRATION

I had the easy part of the assignment: Jim Howe wrote a wonderful first story, and my job was to tell the flip side. Jim's characters were my inspiration; they were already very complete, but I knew we needed to see Alex's family in my story. Because Sally, the pregnant girl, is a rather mysterious presence in Jim's story—and I liked her a lot—I wanted to give her a bigger role in my story as Alex's brother's girlfriend. Playing off Jim's story was so much fun—like putting together a puzzle long-distance!

Rita Williams-Garcia has been a groundbreaking young adult author since the late 1980s. Her characters have sass and inner yearnings, and her writer's voice allows them exceptional reach. She never cowers from saying exactly what her stories drive her to say. In novels like *Every Time a Rainbow Dies, Jumped,* and *No Laughter Here,* her courageous voice is unwavering. She has been challenged in many states, acclaimed in many more; she was awarded the PEN/Norma Klein Citation for Children's Literature in 1991 and again in 1997. Her book *One Crazy Summer* was a National Book Award Finalist, a 2011 Coretta Scott King Award Winner, a 2011 Newbery Honor Book, and won the 2011 Scott O'Dell Award for Historical Fiction. Williams-Garcia continues to break stereotypical mindsets through talent and courage. Her story about interracial dating, paired with Printz Honor author Terry Trueman's story, continues in that proud, lyrical tradition. *www.ritawg.com*

Terry Trueman was a poet and teacher in Seattle and Spokane, Washington, before he became a young adult novelist—a dyed-in-the-wool bohemian like his idol Charles Bukowski before him. He fell in love and married the mother of his son Sheehan, who was born—due to medical error—with cerebral palsy and the physical and mental incapacities that sometimes go with it, and still, he wrote heartbreaking poetry. But when he transformed his son's story into *Stuck in Neutral*, a Printz Honor–winning young adult concept novel, his career paths shifted, and he became a fiction writer full-time. *Inside Out, No Right Turn, Hurricane*, and other novels soon followed. His short story for this collection is one more step down that winding professional road. Today he lives with his wife, Patty, and her sister Donna in Spokane. He hears regularly from his second son, Jesse, now living and working in Los Angeles.

www.terrytrueman.com

TRUEMAN'S INSPIRATION

As the parent of an adopted Hispanic son and because I actually was born in Birmingham, Alabama—I've always had strong feelings about race and diversity in American culture. I grew up in Seattle, but in a part of the city—the northern suburbs—with virtually NO ethnic diversity. The chance to work with Rita, a writer I admire greatly and who also happens to be black, inspired my story—an interracial dating piece without enormous tension or drama, because it's set in what I hope is an ever-improving and more tolerant world.

Terry Davis grew up in Spokane, Washington, a sturdy, solid athlete of good nature—a wrestler of heart and determination who prized his balance as much as he did his skill with thoughts and words. After he studied under John Irving at the University of Iowa's Writers' Workshop and completed a Wallace Stegner Literary Fellowship at Stanford, he taught other eager students and began to write *Vision Quest*, an American Book Award Nominee that launched his career. He has since written two other novels, *If*

Rock and Roll Were a Machine and *Mysterious Ways*, along with many acclaimed short stories, including his contribution to this anthology with his former wife, Rebecca Fjelland Davis. He took an early retirement from the MFA program at Minnesota State University at Mankato and now lives in a cabin on the banks of Loon Lake, near Spokane, where he feels endlessly inspired. *www.writerterrydavis.com*

DAVIS'S INSPIRATION

Each pair of stories in this anthology is about bridging the gap of gender-based misunderstanding with the most reliable of human structures—the truth. Each team of writers deftly illustrates the courage required to ask, "What is really happening here?" and, more important, to ask why.

Rebecca Fjelland Davis spent a lifetime as an avid but critical reader, student, and teacher. Besides her family, her loves are stories, cycling, animals, and the family farm. When she wrote *Jake Riley: Irreparably Damaged*, her first young adult novel in 2003, and a BCCB Blue Ribbon Book in Fiction, she drew from her combined experiential base to secure a voice that was seasoned and convincing. She brings that same library of sensibilities to *Chasing AllieCat*, her 2011 novel, a Junior Library Guild Selection and a Loft-McKnight Children's Honor book, as well as to her contribution to this anthology—a new voice with a knowledge tried and true. *www.rebeccafjellanddavis.com*

FJELLAND DAVIS'S INSPIRATION

I wanted to write a story that protested the government's lifting of restrictions on hog factories—in such a way that we might care about a character involved and then perhaps care about the issue. Kerry was a natural character, and lo and behold, she was in love with a beautiful Muslim boy who can't eat pork. The result was that their relationship became the pivotal point for the story.

Sara Ryan, like Ellen Wittlinger, was a librarian before she was a published writer. Tagged to participate in gifted educational programs most of her life, Ryan was raised a prodigy, with good cause. Her first novel, *Empress of the World* exploded into the young adult literary community as the new voice, giving hope to lesbian teens across the country. She lives and creates with her comic book illustrator/graphic novelist husband, Steve Lieber, in Portland, Oregon. And she remains a librarian—one who writes award-winning fiction, including the Flytrap comic book series, on the side. Her partner in this anthology, Randy Powell, is her longstanding mentor and friend.

www.sararyan.com

Randy Powell has lived on "the coast," also known as Seattle, Washington, since 1956, also known as his entire life. As a kid, he was a sports fan, playing football and tennis. As an adult, he became a writer of fiction heralded for his firm grip on humor and the true voice of America's family life in such works as *Tribute to Another Dead Rock Star*, *Is Kissing a Girl Who Smokes Like Licking an Ashtray?* and *Run If You Dare*. Because he and his wife are raising two sons in the rain forests of Washington State, his life is an authentic research base. But he admits he's happy his family is a little less troubled than some of the characters he's so deftly penned.

www.randypowell.com

POWELL'S INSPIRATION

There are a couple of girls I knew when I was a young kid. I've lost touch with them, and I sometimes wonder whatever happened to them, whether they're even alive or not. That was the spark for this story.